contents

For Madeline.
—A.B.U.

EVEN MORE SCARY MYSTERIES FOR SLEEP-OVERS

By Allen B. Ury
Illustrated by Mia Tavonatti

An RGA Book
PRICE STERN SLOAN
Los Angeles

Copyright © 1997 RGA Publishing Group, Inc.
Published by Price Stern Sloan, Inc.
A member of The Putnam & Grosset Group, New York, New York.

ISBN: 0-8431-7956-2
First Edition
1 3 5 7 9 10 8 6 4 2

Library of Congress Cataloging-in-Publication Data

Ury, Allen B.
    Even more scary mysteries for sleep-overs / by Allen B. Ury ;
illustrated by Mia Tavonatti.
        p.   cm.
    "RGA book."
    Contents: A lotto murder—Live and learn—Checkmate—Call me Jody
—Stringer—Body donor—The beacon—Exclusive interview—Bear facts
—The mother lode.
    Summary: Ten spooky stories with bone-chilling twists.
    ISBN 0-8431-7956-2
    1. Horror tales, American. 2. Children's stories, American.
[1. Horror stories. 2. Short stories.] I. Tavonatti, Mia, ill.
II. Title.
PZ7.U694Ev   1997   96-30547
[Fic]--dc20   CIP
                                                                  AC

checkmate

Russell Varney walked slowly down Buchanan Avenue checking the street addresses against the number he'd written on a piece of notepaper. The phone call had been very specific. He was to meet his friend in front of 566 Buchanan Avenue at exactly 4:00 P.M. to discuss "a matter of life or death." Although Russell was aware that his friend was prone to exaggeration, the tension in his friend's voice told him that this meeting probably was pretty important.

With a full minute to spare, Russell found himself standing in front of 566 Buchanan Avenue, which turned out to be a pawnshop. Why would his friend pick such an odd place to meet? Usually when they got together, it was at the mall or a fast food place.

Nervously, he checked his watch. It was exactly four o'clock, but his friend was nowhere in sight. Starting to get impatient, Russell suddenly heard something move above him, and when he looked up he saw three large brass spheres hanging directly overhead. Each about the size of a basketball, he recognized these spheres as the ancient symbol for *pawnbroker*. Now someone was moving around among the wires that held these balls in place, although his position prevented Russell from seeing who it was.

Before Russell could figure out what was happening, he heard something go *snap!* and a moment later the three balls came crashing down on him. He barely had a chance to cry out before one of the spheres hit him on the top of the head with a loud *thunk!* His body instantly convulsed, then fell lifelessly to the sidewalk.

■ ■ ■ ■

The next morning the entire student body of Niles Junior High was called to the school's auditorium where the principal grimly announced the death of Russell Varney to the stunned crowd. Toni Lorring was particularly shocked and saddened by the news. She and Russell had been members of the school's prize-winning chess club since the sixth grade. They had spent many an afternoon huddled over a red-and-black-squared gameboard locked in a stirring battle of wits. Now she would never ever see him again.

That afternoon, Toni and the fifteen other chess club members gathered in the science classroom where they met every Tuesday and Thursday, and the first thing on everyone's lips was the death of Russell Varney.

"It's so strange," noted Patti Conroy, who, as always, was wearing one of her mother's hand-knit sweaters. "I mean, what are the odds of being accidentally killed by a falling pawnshop symbol? One in a zillion?"

"Maybe it wasn't exactly an accident," suggested Reggie Bartholomew, nervously twirling a plastic ballpoint pen between his fingers.

"Who would want to kill Russell?" Ross Slotten objected. Russell had been one of Ross's best friends, and the boy's death had hit him particularly hard. "And if someone *did* want to kill him, there had to be a simpler way to do it."

"Fellow chess players," Toni said grimly. "I suggest that we dedicate the rest of this year's competitions to the memory of Russell Varney, chess player extraordinaire."

The other players voiced their agreement then broke out the chessboards to begin their weekly games.

■ ■ ■ ■

Patti Conroy received the call just minutes after she'd gotten home from school. Her friend had asked her to meet him over by Buckman's cornfield right away. It was, in his words, "a matter of life or death."

Now, standing with her bike just off the narrow asphalt road that ran along the cornfield, Patti began to wonder why her friend had chosen such a strange, out-of-the-way place to meet. From where she stood, she couldn't see another living soul. The only obvious signs of life were a dozen or so huge, black crows circling overhead.

For a moment, Patti thought about Russell Varney's awful death and shivered. Still upset over recent events and feeling slightly paranoid, she was checking her watch impatiently when she heard a rustling sound in the tall corn behind her. Spinning around, she thought she saw a dark form moving among the large, leafy stalks.

"Hello?" she called, moving closer to the field's edge. "Is that you?"

Suddenly, someone leaped out of the cornfield holding a large plastic bucket. Giving a high-pitched "Aiiieee!," he hurled the bucket's contents directly at her. A split second later, Patti was hit by what felt like a load of wet sand. But when the dust cleared, her coughing subsided, and she brushed her eyes clear, she saw that she was covered with a strange, powdery yellow substance. It took her a moment to recognize it, and when she did, she was more confused than ever.

"This is cornmeal, you idiot!" she cried. "You called me out here to cover me with *cornmeal?* What are you—*completely out of your mind?*"

"Checkmate!" her attacker replied with a sly smile, then backed up into the row of stalks, vanishing from sight before Patti ever saw who had pulled this bizarre stunt.

Patti just stood there, looking like a yellow ghost, trying in vain to understand why this was happening to her. She was still standing there by the roadside when she heard the loud *caw!* of one of the circling crows. Before she could even look up, one of the birds swooped in and pecked several times at her head before flying off.

"Ouch!" Patti screamed, flailing her arms wildly. "Get away from me!"

Then two more crows swooped in and stabbed at her with their sharp beaks. Patti shrieked at the top of her lungs and turned to run. But because she was blinded by the frantic beating of the birds' wings, she tripped and fell face-first to the

muddy ground. Within seconds, the entire flock was upon her, their claws digging into her skin as they pecked away at the cornmeal covering her from head to toe.

■ ■ ■ ■

"Patti Conroy was . . . *pecked to death*?" Toni Lorring cried in disbelief. "That's awful! How could a thing like that ever happen?"

"She was over by Buckman's cornfield and a bunch of crows decided to have her for lunch," Reggie Bartholomew replied. They were standing at their lockers before class.

"It sounds like something out of a horror movie," Mark Miter said with a grimace from three lockers away. Mark had been one of the chess club's top players until three months ago when he flunked history and was banned from participating in extracurricular activities until his grades improved. His loss had been a blow to the club. They had been counting on Mark to lead them to victory in the recent All-City Chess Tournament. As it turned out, their team still won the junior high/middle school-level championship—but just barely. "What an awful way to go, don't you think?" he added with a shudder.

"You realize this makes *two* chess club members who have died under mysterious circumstances in the last few days?" Toni said anxiously. "What are the odds of *that* being a coincidence?"

"Astronomical," Mark said with a worried look.

"Which means that maybe they *weren't* accidents," Reggie replied, swallowing nervously. "Maybe someone is out to kill all of us!"

"Well, personally, I think you're being a little paranoid," Mark said. "But if you want, I could ask my cousin Pete for some advice. He used to be a private detective."

10

"I'm going straight to the police," Toni announced. "If someone *is* trying to knock off all the chess club members, he has to be stopped before he strikes again!"

■ ■ ■ ■

Reggie Bartholomew was caught completely by surprise. One minute he was walking through the medieval arts exhibit at the city's World History Museum. The next, he was lying dead beneath a 150-pound suit of armor that had mysteriously toppled off its pedestal just as he was walking by.

"Checkmate," a voice had whispered from the shadows just before the whole thing happened. It was the same voice that had called Reggie to the museum in the first place. It was a voice Reggie had known for many years, which he'd trusted with his life. Now, the mysterious figure turned and hurried away. There were still many moves to make before this particular chess game was over.

■ ■ ■ ■

"The killer has to be one of us," Toni said grimly as she moved her white knight to capture her opponent's black rook that Thursday afternoon. All of the chess club members had spent much of the previous day being interviewed by the local police, but none of them had been able to provide any solid leads as to who the killer might be. After that, several parents had forced their kids to quit the club until the killer was caught, and now its membership was down to a mere six—including Toni herself. Although Toni knew her life was probably in danger, she didn't

11

believe that simply quitting an afterschool club was going to stop the murderer if he was truly intent on killing her.

"Why do you think it's one of us?" Andy Rodgers asked, moving his queen into a position that trapped Toni's knight. Andy was not only the quarterback for the school's football team, he was also one of the best players in the chess club. He had a particular talent for being able to think three or four moves ahead during a game. This made him an almost unbeatable opponent both on the football field and behind the chessboard. Like Toni, Andy believed that the club should continue to meet despite the recent deaths—or perhaps even because of them. As he'd put it, "Russell, Patti, and Reggie would have wanted it this way."

Now Toni carefully studied the board and considered her position, both in the game in front of her as well as the one being played out in real life. "All three victims were members of this group," she explained. "Each of them was killed in a place they wouldn't normally go. This suggests that they were lured there—lured there by someone they trusted. And who are you more likely to trust than one of your own?"

She now moved her bishop to counter the threat of Andy's queen. Andy saw that he was vulnerable and immediately moved his queen back to a more defendable position.

"Plus, look closely at the pattern," Toni continued as she considered her next move. "Russell was killed outside a pawnshop. Patti was killed by crows, one type of which is called a rook. And Reggie was crushed by a suit of armor."

"Pawn, rook, and knight," Andy said, now realizing where his friend was headed. "All chess pieces."

"The method is painfully obvious," Toni said as she moved a pawn forward on the board. It looked liked a pointless move, but she was setting a trap she expected Andy to fall into three turns from now. "The question is, what's the motive? Why kill us off? If we can answer that one, then chances are we'll have our murder suspect."

Andy smiled, and captured Toni's pawn with his bishop. Suddenly, Toni's king was trapped with absolutely no place to go. This meant that Toni had lost the game. "Checkmate," he said, smiling pleasantly.

Toni had never seen it coming.

■ ■ ■ ■

"I think I know who the killer is!" Mark Miter cried excitedly into the phone.

"Who?" Toni asked, pacing around her bedroom with her cordless phone pressed to her ear.

"Well, first of all, it's not who you might think," Mark replied. "And second of all, I need to tell you in person. Can you meet me over at McQueen's Point in fifteen minutes? I think I have the proof we've been looking for."

"All right," Toni agreed. "Fifteen minutes." She stood in silence for a long moment, listening to the dial tone. Then she quickly dialed another number.

■ ■ ■ ■

Mark Miter was waiting for her by the safety railing when Toni arrived at the McQueen's Point lookout a quarter of an hour later. Located at the top of a cliff with a one-hundred-foot-high drop-off, McQueen's Point was a favorite spot for bird-watchers and nature lovers.

"Thanks for coming," Mark said anxiously. "Sorry to call you to such an out-of-the-way place, but the truth is, I think I'm being followed."

"By whom? The killer?" Toni asked in surprise.

Mark nodded and motioned her toward the bench.

"I've spent the last few days digging around, trying to see if I could come up with a pattern to the deaths," he began.

"I already know the pattern," Toni interrupted. "Pawn, rook, knight. They're all chess pieces, in ascending order of importance—from the weakest to the most powerful."

"And what does that tell us?" Mark asked, leading her on.

"That the killer is a chess player. Maybe even a very good one," Toni replied. "It also tells me who the next victim will be."

"Who?" Mark asked anxiously.

"Me," Toni announced flatly.

For a moment, Mark just sat there with his jaw hanging open in shock. Then he jumped to his feet and grabbed Toni by the hand. "We've got to get you out of here," he insisted. "We can't let Andy get you."

"Andy *Rodgers*?" Toni said in surprise. "You think Andy's the killer?"

"Of course I do," Mark said with conviction. "Whoever pulled off those murders had to be pretty strong. I mean, how many kids do you know who could cut the cable on a pawnbroker's sign or push over a hundred and fifty pound suit of armor? Andy's the biggest guy on the team. He's the only one who could have done it."

"Maybe—but then, maybe not," Toni countered. "Anyone with the right tools could have done those things. Plus, remember, the chess pieces were in *reverse* order of importance. That means the next murder will involve a bishop."

"So how does that rule out Andy?" Mark asked, confused.

"Look where we are," Toni said. "McQueen's Point. This is where I'm supposed to be killed."

"But you just said you'd be killed with a bishop," Mark reminded her.

"No, not with a bishop," Toni explained. "By a bishop. Isn't that right, Mr. Miter?"

"Toni, I don't have the slightest idea what you're talking about," Mark said, eyeing her warily.

"According to the dictionary, a miter is the pointed hat worn by Catholic clerics, like bishops," Toni explained. "You're the killer, Mark. We all know how upset you were about being kicked out of the chess club. Although that wasn't our fault, you still hated the fact that we managed to win the All-City Championship without you. Suddenly, you felt like you weren't important. That you didn't count. And your ego couldn't take that. You had to somehow prove that you were the cleverest and most powerful one of us all."

"Well done, Toni," Mark said coldly, suddenly gripping her wrist with his hand. "But this game isn't over. I still have one move left."

Far taller and stronger than Toni, Mark had no problem dragging her over to the guardrail and leaning her body over the precipice below.

"It's a tragic story. Young teen, walking alone, slips and falls to her death over a cliff," he said with a chilling laugh. "I'm sure the chess club will feel very sorry about losing you—for about five minutes—just like they felt so sorry about losing me!"

Taking a deep breath, he prepared to heave Toni over the railing when he was suddenly caught in a blinding searchlight.

"Hold it right there, Mark!" a voice ordered over an amplified bullhorn. "Let the girl go, step away, and keep your hands in plain sight!"

15

"I thought this might be a trap as soon as you mentioned McQueen's Point," Toni explained, gasping for breath as soon as Mark released her. "At first I was confused by the fact that the bishop seemed to be missing from the murder pattern. But then I remembered the meaning of your name, and it all came together. That's when I called the police. You should know," Toni smiled, "in order to win this game, you have to think at least two moves ahead."

stringer

Some people don't decide on a career until they're well out of school. Others know right from the start what they want to do with their lives. You might say they have a calling.

Howard Stadlin was one of these kids. Although he was only an eighth grader, Howard knew he was going to be a TV newsman when he grew up. Not just some third-string reporter working for station WZYZ in Podunk, Iowa, not some second-rate network correspondent assigned to Outer Nowhereland. No, Howard Stadlin was going to be a network anchorman. He was going to be a star. He was going to *be* the evening news.

While other kids plastered their bedroom walls with posters of rock stars and sports heroes, Howard had his room decorated with framed photos of Peter Jennings, Tom Brokaw,

Dan Rather, Bernard Shaw, Ted Koppel, and Stone Phillips. I mean, Howard took TV news as seriously as other kids took comic book collecting or choosing the right athletic shoes.

I was amazed at Howard's single-minded determination. Heck, I was still deciding whether to be a cowboy or an astronaut when I grew up. And watching Howard map out his life, plotting exactly where he'd be at five-year intervals, filled me with awe.

"How do you know that all these things will happen exactly when you say they will?" I once asked him as we sat together at lunch, his life plan laid out between us. "I mean, I don't even know what I'm having for *dinner* tonight!"

"It's easy, Bob. I'm going to *make* them happen," Howard replied with complete seriousness. "A professional sets his goals, then does everything necessary to achieve them."

"I think a lot of it is just, you know, being in the right place at the right time."

"I say, dumb luck is for losers, Bobby-boy," Howard replied. "Professionals make their own luck."

"How?" I asked.

"Preparation. Education. Perseverance," he said as if reading a message off some kind of silly motivational poster. "P-E-P!"

"You know something, Howard," I said, taking a bite of my turkey-on-rye sandwich, "you're scary."

"You ain't seen nothin' yet," Howard said with a look in his eye that was so cold it could freeze hot lava.

■ ■ ■ ■

The following Wednesday morning, Howard bounded into our homeroom class wearing the biggest grin I'd ever seen.

"What happened, Howard? You win the lottery?" I asked.

"Even better, Bobby-boy," Howard replied. "I'm working for Channel 5 News."

"You're kidding!" I gasped in disbelief. "You mean like you're working in the mailroom?"

"No, bonehead. As a *reporter*!" he announced.

"No way!" I exclaimed. "How did you swing that? You're only thirteen years old! What did you do, get a fake ID? Tell 'em you're a midget?"

"I'm working as a *stringer*," Howard said. "That means I look for news stories, then phone them into the station."

"So you're not an actual reporter then," I corrected him. "You're not really working for a station. And you don't actually report *on camera*—"

"That will happen soon enough," Howard insisted as if he had his own private window on the future. "This is my foot in the door. Within three months I'll be writing actual news copy. And three months after that I'll have done my first on-camera spot. Just wait."

Knowing Howard Stadlin as well as I did, I wasn't going to bet against him.

■ ■ ■ ■

Two days after becoming a Channel 5 stringer, Howard had his first report appear on the air. A car had back-ended a mail truck, causing hundreds of letters to spill all over Tenth Avenue. Howard happened to be riding by on his bike at the time and immediately called the station from a nearby pay phone. Then, flashing his Channel 5 ID card like a police badge, he went about interviewing the driver of the car, the mail carrier, and the motorcycle cop who showed up to investigate the accident.

19

When the on-air reporter and her video crew finally arrived fifteen minutes later, Howard had all his notes recopied and ready for her to use. Although the incident had occurred late in the afternoon, Howard's preparation was so complete that the reporter was able to shoot, edit, and have her piece ready to air on the six o'clock news.

"And this is just the beginning," he told me the next day.

Once again, Howard spoke the truth. Over the course of the next month, he phoned in an average of one story per day. According to the deal he made with Channel 5, he got paid $25 for each of his stories they covered, and an additional $25 if the story actually made it on the air. Most of these stories were sensationalistic news items, such as freeway crashes, house fires, and various local arrests. And when there weren't any big crimes or disasters to report, Howard went out looking for human interest items. One time he found a former homeless person who went on to found a successful computer software company. Another time he found a man who claimed to have the world's largest bottle cap collection. On average, the station sent a reporter out to cover one out of every three stories Howard phoned in. Of those, about three out of five made it on the air. Consequently, for a thirteen-year-old, Howard was making a pretty good living, not to mention preparing himself for his eventual adult career.

"Mr. Wagner—he's the station's assignment editor—told me I'm the most productive stringer he has," Howard boasted over lunch. "In fact, starting next week he's going to list me on the closing credits as a contributing writer."

"That's great," I said, shaking my head in wonder. "You're ahead of your life plan by at least three weeks . . . "

"I know, but there's just one problem," Howard said darkly. "Mr. Wagner says I can't be an official news writer because I'm too young to join the labor union. And he won't let me do any on-air reporting, because no one's going to accept the news coming from a kid."

I could hear the bitterness in Howard's voice. Here he was working harder than most people twice his age, and he was being denied career advancement because of factors over which he had no control. According to Howard, it was nothing but blatant age discrimination!

"Hey, I've got an idea," I said, having a sudden flash of inspiration. "Why don't you tell them you'll just cover junior high and grammar school news? You know, current events from a kid's perspective. They could make it like a weekly feature."

"Good thinking, Bobby-boy!" Howard exclaimed, slapping me on the back. "I'll suggest it to Mr. Wagner first thing after school today!"

Howard's boss liked the idea and agreed to let him tape a sample report. Howard decided to do his story on a recent rash of bicycle thefts at our junior high. Using my dad's 8mm camcorder for the assignment, with me as his cameraman, he interviewed about a half-dozen kids who'd had their bikes stolen during the past month. We then headed over to the police station where Howard questioned the local police chief about what he was doing to find the thief.

Then Howard got an idea. He had us hide out in some bushes near the main bike rack so we could catch the thieves in the act. Sure enough, less than an hour later, three high school drop-outs showed up with a big set of wire cutters and proceeded to steal two mountain bikes. We got the whole thing on tape. Not only did Howard's piece make the evening news, but our tape was used to help arrest the responsible teenagers.

Now Howard was on the fast track to TV news stardom. His reports aired at least once a week, covering everything from our championship swim team to the newest ways students had devised to cheat on tests.

But still Howard wasn't satisfied.

"I'm never going to get anywhere doing these stupid puff pieces," he grumbled one day after we'd taped a story about how student demands were changing the types of food being served in the cafeteria. "I should be covering hard news. Fires. Crime. Political corruption."

"Well, why don't we start sniffing around?" I suggested. "Remember the bike theft piece we did? Maybe we can uncover a gang selling counterfeit meal tickets or something like that."

That idea lay unrealized, more or less, until three days later. It was eight o'clock on a Tuesday night. I was getting ready to sit down and watch my favorite TV sitcom when my telephone rang. Howard was on the line. He was calling from school.

"Get your camcorder down here, pronto!" he said. "We have a hot story to do!"

"What could be going on at school at eight o'clock at night?" I asked.

"A fire!" he announced.

Five minutes later, I braked my bike to a stop in front of our building's main entrance. Fire trucks were just arriving on the scene. No other news crews had shown up yet.

"Hurry!" Howard shouted, directing me over to position my camera directly in front of the burning first-floor room. He grabbed the microphone that was wired to my camera, quickly brushed back his hair, then waited until I had turned on the battery-powered light.

"Go!" I said, properly framing him against the scene of firefighters at work.

"A fire broke out here at Robert Goddard Junior High at approximately 7:55 this evening," Howard began in his most authoritative voice. "Although investigators have yet to determine the cause of the blaze, which gutted at least one classroom on the building's first floor, it is believed that arson may be involved. . . . "

■ ■ ■ ■

Howard's report was the lead item on Channel 5's ten o'clock news that night. Because he and I were the first newspeople on the scene, we were able to scoop every other station in town, getting our report on before anyone else. I have to admit, I was *very* proud of our work.

When it was all over, I asked Howard how he managed to learn about the fire before anyone else.

"I bought a police scanner," he explained. "It picks up all the emergency calls. And since I live just two blocks away, I was able to get here before the regular news crews."

Howard's explanation made perfect sense to me. But there were some kids at school who had other ideas. After the police investigators concluded that the fire had indeed been started by someone throwing a homemade gasoline bomb through the window, the rumor began to circulate that Howard had actually done the deed himself. Kids were saying that he was so desperate to be a big-shot reporter that he'd begun *making* news so he could be the first to report it.

I tried to tell these guys that they were wrong—that Howard simply had good reporter's instincts—but the stories kept going around the school. And things only got worse after Howard was the first one on the scene of another fire at an abandoned warehouse in the River District, which was also caused by arson.

23

"That friend of yours is nuts," one of my lifelong buddies, Brandon Hayes, told me just before math class. "One of these days, he's going to get someone killed—if he isn't arrested first. I'd stay as far away from him as possible if I were you."

The fact was, by this time, Howard was working almost full-time with one of Channel 5's tape crews, so I really wasn't seeing all that much of him anyway. Even so, hearing people accuse him of committing crimes just to further his own career made me realize that I'd have to settle this issue once and for all.

■ ■ ■ ■

I heard the call over my uncle's police-band radio shortly after sundown. Supposedly, someone was using the equipment in our junior high chemistry lab to rig a bomb big enough to blow up the whole building. Although more than a dozen print, radio, and TV reporters were now covering the story, only one had actually gotten inside the building. And that one intrepid journalist was none other than thirteen-year-old Howard Stadlin.

Knowing that the source of Howard's uncanny success would have to be exposed sooner or later, I sat crouched behind a lab bench, watching the red and white police lights play off the walls. Soon the truth—the *real* truth—would be known to all.

Hearing the science lab door open, I spun around and saw a familiar form framed in the doorway.

"Hello, Howard," I said with a smile. "Fancy meeting you here, my friend."

"Bob, what the heck are you doing here?" Howard cried, clearly caught by surprise.

"You're the reporter, you tell me," I responded, trying to stay calm.

24

"It looks like you're getting ready to blow up the school," Howard said. "Otherwise, you tell *me* why you're standing there with what looks like a homemade bomb."

"You're wrong," I replied, unable to suppress a giggle rising in my throat. "It doesn't just look like a homemade bomb—it *is* a homemade bomb. No one becomes a hero for preventing a *fake* bomb from going off, right?"

"I don't know why you're doing this, but I think you should come with me, Bob," Howard said, trying to stay cool, calm, and professional.

"You don't know why I'm doing this?" I asked in surprise. "It should be obvious. I'm doing it for the same reason I threw that gasoline bomb into the school two weeks ago, then set that warehouse fire."

"*You* caused those fires?" Howard gasped in disbelief.

"You said it yourself, you have to make your own luck," I exclaimed. "Heck, I couldn't let you stand around and wait for hot stories to break. That could have taken forever. So I *made* the news happen. And now you're the most famous eighth grader in the whole city! Are we a great team or what?"

"We are not a *team!*" Howard growled. "If I'd known you were behind those fires, I would have turned you in to the cops straightaway."

"Gee, whatever happened to the idea of protecting your sources?" I asked, stung by my friend's betrayal. "Whatever happened to loyalty?"

"Look, we can talk about this some other time," Howard said, motioning me toward the door. "Right now, I think we should leave and let the bomb squad disarm this thing."

"First, aren't you going to interview me?" I asked eagerly, my right hand poised over the detonating switch. "That's why I asked for you. I'm giving you the exclusive. You'll be the only reporter in town who got to speak face-to-face with the Junior High Bomber."

"All right, Bob." Howard said, cautiously taking out his microcassette recorder. "Let's talk."

■ ■ ■ ■

Howard's interview with me lasted almost a full hour, but only a few seconds of it ever made it onto the Channel 5 News. The story about my plot to make my friend a journalistic superstar, however, was picked up by the national wire services. In fact, soon practically every newspaper, magazine, and TV station in the country was asking to interview *him*.

All that attention led to over a dozen magazine covers, Howard's own national reporting spot, and finally a scholarship to study journalism at a major Midwestern university. Today, if you ever watch the Satellite News Network, you know that Howard Stadlin is a first-string TV journalist, usually covering crime stories on the East Coast. He's not an anchorman yet, but you can bet he will be someday.

Me, I watch him as often as I can. I'm lucky this mental hospital gets cable. At least now I don't have to worry about what I'm going to do when *I* grow up . . . because they say I'm going to be in here a long, long time. . . .

bear facts

licia Tagliabu grabbed Georgia Solo's arm. "Stop!" she shouted. "I have to go into that store!"

Alicia and Georgia were walking through the small commercial district on Downer Avenue on their way home from Ramona Junior High School when they noticed that a brand-new store had opened in the middle of the block. The shop had a false-brick facade that made it look like a miniature European castle. The fancy Olde English lettering above the door read BEAR FACTS, and a colorful banner stretched over its windows declared GRAND OPENING! Behind the polished glass sat more than a dozen fancy-dressed teddy bears.

"You've got to be kidding," Georgia scoffed. "That's a *toy* store. You know, for little kids. You're twelve years old—almost a teenager. I mean, come on, Alicia! You're too big to be playing with teddy bears!"

"I don't play with them, I *collect* them," Alicia explained. The girls shared several classes together, but only recently they had become friends outside of school. "You know, the same way some people collect porcelain dolls or model trains. It's a hobby. Come on. Let's take a look."

When the girls walked in, they were immediately surrounded by teddy bears. There were bears on benches, on the walls, and even hanging from the ceiling. There were bears of all shapes and sizes—some no larger than a ball, while others were as tall as the girls themselves. There were brown bears and black bears, green bears and tan bears, red, white, and blue bears, and bears the colors of the rainbow. Some were dressed like doctors, some like ballerinas, and some like tennis players. In fact, Alicia was sure she was seeing more bears here than she'd ever seen in one place in her entire life. And, being an avid bear collector, she'd seen plenty.

"Why, hello, girls," a sweet-looking older gentleman said as he appeared out of a back room. "Welcome to Bear Facts. I'm the owner of this establishment, Mr. Bear." He chuckled. "Yes, that's my real name. And in case you haven't guessed, I sell teddy bears!"

"Gee, I never would have guessed," Georgia said rolling her eyes at this corny old guy.

"Is there a special kind of a bear you're looking for?" Mr. Bear asked, peering over his half-rimmed glasses. "A special color? A certain texture? Perhaps one with a unique personality? We have all kinds."

"Yes, I can see that," Alicia said as she strolled past the shelves overflowing with stuffed bears. And then the oddest feeling came over her. It was like she could hear a voice speaking directly inside her head. *Over here!* it called. *I'm the one you're looking for!*

Stopping dead in her tracks, Alicia pulled a bear off the shelf directly in front of her. Compared to all the custom-dressed bears around it, this one looked pretty ordinary. About fourteen inches tall and covered with soft gray fur, it had leather pads for hands and feet, and a plush brown muzzle. If the bear had any one distinguishing feature, it was its eyes. They were bright blue and had an almost liquid quality to them, making the bear look practically alive. In fact, Alicia had never before seen a toy with such alert, hypnotic eyes. Had this bear actually spoken to her? she wondered. Or was it just a trick of the mind? Either way, she knew she *had* to have it.

"How much for this one?" she asked.

Mr. Bear walked over and examined the small cardboard tag hanging from the stuffed animal's foot. "Fourteen ninety-five," he replied with a grin. "Quite a bargain, I'd say."

"I'll take it," Alicia said, reaching for her purse.

"You're kidding," Georgia gasped. "For me, that's more than two weeks of allowance!"

"For me, too," Alicia admitted. "But I've got to have that bear for my room."

"Wow, I've got to see that room of yours," Georgia exclaimed.

"Well, come on over," Alicia said as she put her money on the counter. "And get ready to be impressed!"

■ ■ ■ ■

"Wow, you weren't kidding when you said you collected teddy bears!" Georgia exclaimed as she stepped into Alicia's bedroom. All done up in pink and white, featuring lace curtains and a canopied bed, the room was covered with teddy bears. On the bed, on the dresser, and piled in the corner, the bears were everywhere. In fact, there seemed to be as many bears here as there were at the Bear Facts shop. "How long have you been doing this?" Georgia asked in awe.

"Well, I got my first bear two months before I was born, and the collection's been growing ever since!" Alicia said with a laugh as she set her new gray bear on her bed along with a half-dozen others. "In fact, according to my parents, my first word was 'bear!'"

"And I bet you've given each of them a name, right?" Georgia asked as she looked over the sea of adorable furry faces and glassy eyes.

"Of course," Alicia said. "There's Barry, and Boris, and Brenda, and Bartholomew—"

"What are you going to do when you run out of B's?" asked Georgia, sensing a pattern.

"I already did," Alicia replied. She turned around and began naming off the bears on the other side of the room. "There's Teddy, and Todd, and Terri, and Thomasina. . . . "

She stopped and turned to her newest acquisition. Again, its glistening eyes seemed to stare right back at her, and she could swear she heard a voice—a distant voice—speaking directly into her mind. *Georgia*, it said. *Call me Georgia.*

"And I'll call this one—Georgia!" she declared, staring deeply into her new bear's eyes.

"I'm flattered," Georgia said dryly. "Just one thing. How do you manage to sleep in here with all these eyeballs staring at you? Personally, they'd give me the creeps."

Alicia looked over the expanse of unblinking eyes staring at her from every corner of her bedroom. She'd never thought of these bears as scary before, but now that Georgia mentioned it, all those furry faces angled directly toward her bed did seem a bit, well, threatening.

"Come on," she said, quickly shaking off the uncomfortable feeling that had suddenly come over her. "I'll show you the rest of the house."

As the girls turned to go, Alicia took one last look back at her newest bear. For the briefest instant, she thought she saw its right arm move. The movement had been slight, almost imperceptible, but she was sure she'd seen it. Well, *almost* sure. And then, as she continued to stare at the bear, searching for even the slightest sign of additional movement, she realized how foolish she must look and scolded herself for acting childishly. Heck, these bears were nothing but cloth, plastic, and stuffing, she thought. What harm could they possibly do?

■ ■ ■ ■

When Alicia awoke the next morning, she knew immediately that something was wrong. At first, there was nothing she could put her finger on. She just had a very uneasy feeling.

But a minute or two after climbing out of bed, she realized what the problem was. Some of her bears had been moved. Every night before going to sleep, she took the bears that sat on her bed and set them on the floor by the closet door. But now the bears weren't there. Instead, they'd been moved to different positions all around the room. One was on her dresser. Another was on the window seat. Two more were sitting by her bedroom door. And the gray bear she'd purchased the day before was lying on the floor directly beside her bed.

"Mom, did you or Dad come into my room last night and move my bears around?" Alicia asked as she entered the kitchen.

"Of course not," her mother said. "Why would we do a thing like that?"

"I don't know," Alicia said, taking a sip of orange juice. "But somebody did. When I woke up this morning, they weren't where I put them last night."

"Ooooo-WEEEEE-ooooo!" her dad joked, making weird science fiction sounds. "It sounds to me like you were visited by alien interior decorators!"

"This isn't funny, Dad!" Alicia snapped. "Those bears didn't move by themselves. Someone was in my room!" It would have been convenient for Alicia to blame her little brother or kid sister for this. But being an only child, Alicia didn't *have* a little brother or kid sister. That left only her parents or . . . *ghosts?* It was a possibility Alicia didn't even want to consider.

"Maybe you got up in the middle of the night and moved them in your sleep," her mother suggested. "My Aunt Sylvia was a sleepwalker. Once she walked to the bus stop and took a bus all the way down to 37th Street at two o'clock in the morning. When she woke up standing on the corner, she couldn't remember a thing!"

"They say sleepwalking is hereditary," Alicia's father agreed. "And it certainly makes sense. Tell you what—we'll listen for you tonight. If we hear you walking around in your sleep, we'll let you know," he chuckled good-naturedly.

Alicia didn't believe she was a sleepwalker, but she was ready to accept that explanation before she'd consider the possibility that her house was haunted. The very thought of ghosts had already freaked her out, and just the idea that one might be moving around in her bedroom was enough to make her sleep on the living room couch.

That night Alicia was extremely careful to note exactly where she put her bears before going to bed. She set them neatly in front of her closet door, then did a head count to make sure that all six of them were in place. Then trying to dismiss the idea of ghostly visitors from her mind, she climbed into bed and eventually began drifting off to sleep.

Good night, Alicia, she thought she heard a voice whisper. Bolting up, her heart beating wildly, she looked around the room, but saw that she was still all alone. I must have been dreaming, she thought, struggling to calm herself down. Boy, I'm really letting myself get spooked lately!

Taking a slow, deep breath, Alicia lay back down on her pillow and—after much effort—finally fell asleep.

The next morning, she arose and was at first relieved to find that her six bears were still in front of the closet door . . . until she realized that they'd all changed positions! In fact, Georgia, her newest bear, was now sitting on the shoulders of Beauregard, a large, furry brown bear wearing a cowboy outfit.

Shuddering, Alicia quickly got dressed and hurried downstairs. "Are you *sure* you didn't come into my bedroom last night?" she asked her parents, who were having coffee.

"Why? Did the bears have another party in your room while you were asleep?" her dad asked with a grin.

"This is nothing to joke about, Herbert," Alicia's mother scolded. "She's obviously sleepwalking, just like my Aunt Sylvia does all the time."

But Alicia didn't buy it, and, later that day, neither did her friend Georgia.

"Who in the world moves teddy bears in their sleep?" Georgia said as she and Alicia sat together at lunch. "If you ask me, your parents are playing tricks on you."

"Why would they do *that*?" Alicia inquired.

"They think you're too old to have teddy bears, and they want you to get rid of them," Georgia explained. "This way, by creeping you out, they'll get you to throw them out all on your own."

"That's pretty sick," Alicia responded. "My parents would *never* do something like that."

"Hey, don't take *my* word for it," Georgia said. "When you go to bed tonight, don't let yourself fall asleep. I'll bet you'll see your folks sneak into your room and move a few of your bears around again."

Alicia agreed that this was an excellent plan. That night, she went to bed at her usual time—9:30 P.M.—but instead of falling asleep, she forced herself to stay awake. Around 10:30 she heard her parents starting to get ready for bed. By 11:00 the house was completely silent.

They must figure I'm onto them, Alicia thought. They're not going to try to trick me three nights in a row.

Feeling secure in the knowledge that her bears would not be moved this night, Alicia turned over, took a deep, relaxing breath, and allowed herself to start drifting off to sleep.

She was just starting to slip away when she heard movement somewhere in the room. Instantly her eyes snapped open and her breath caught in her throat. Straining her ears, she heard it again. Something was creeping across the carpet.

Bolting upright, she fumbled for her bedside lamp and switched on the light. Looking wildly about, she saw Georgia, her new toy bear, standing in the center of the room, posed as if it had just been caught in a police spotlight.

"What in the world—?" Alicia began. She threw back her covers, swung her legs around, and reached out toward the fugitive teddy.

"Noooo!" the bear screamed in a strange, high-pitched voice, then bolted for the door. It dashed across the carpeted floor and leaped up for the doorknob, but its plush, padded hands couldn't get a grip on the polished brass handle. A second later, Alicia had the struggling little monster firmly in her grasp.

"Let me go, human!" the bear growled, showing horrifying fangs. "Release me or die!"

Alicia now recognized the voice as the one she thought she'd been hearing in her head. Had this bear, this ordinary stuffed animal, actually been communicating with her?

"Who are you?" Alicia demanded, tightly squeezing the bear's body, which still felt as if it was made out of nothing but cotton stuffing. "I mean, *what* are you?"

"I am an Aldeberaen Paradyne T-1000 Model Twelve Infiltrator," the bear recited robotically. "My brethren and I have been sent to penetrate your world's defenses by inserting ourselves into the homes of your planet's inhabitants."

Alicia's jaw dropped. "You mean, you're from *outer space?*" she gasped in stunned disbelief. "But I bought you from an old man named Mr. Bear!"

"An android designed to look like a native human and aid in our infiltration," the bear replied proudly. "He and his fellow androids have done a remarkable job, wouldn't you say? There are now millions of us in homes throughout your planet. Soon, all humans will be destroyed, making way for the Aldeberaen conquest of Earth."

"Not if I can help it!" Alicia screamed. And with that, she grabbed the teddy bear by its thick, furry legs and slammed it against her dresser over and over again until a seam split across the bear's back and tufts of cottonlike stuffing went streaming into the air. She kept this pounding up until all the fabric innards had been knocked free and the bear was nothing but a collection of ragged pieces. Then, exhausted and gasping for breath, she released the bear's tattered remains and slumped victoriously onto her bed.

"Nice try, Earthling," the bear's head growled, now lying on the floor without its body. "But destroying me alone will be of no use. You see, while I've been here—I've made friends!"

Dropping her jaw, Alicia turned slowly around and saw that now every bear in her bedroom—the black bears, the brown bears, the white bears, and the tanned bears, the bears dressed in clothes, the bears wearing hats, and the bears who wore nothing at all—were all looking directly at her. And then, as one, all the bears smiled, revealing hundreds of sharp, bearlike fangs.

the mother lode

regory Ringold quickly put his finger to his lips and turned to his younger brother, Peter. "Shhhh! I think I just heard something!"

"I hear it, too," twelve-year-old Peter replied in an urgent whisper. "I still hear it." He shuddered. "It sounds like voices! Could those be the ghosts?"

"Maybe," Gregory said, suddenly getting a sick, metallic taste in his mouth. "Something's down in those tunnels, that's for sure."

The Ringold brothers were standing at the entrance to the old Lafferty gold mine, which sat at the end of an overgrown dirt road about three miles south of the mountain community of Lodestone, California. Desperate for some excitement on this

Saturday afternoon, the boys had ignored their parents' warnings to stay away from the long-abandoned mine and decided to check the place out for themselves. Maybe there was still a gold nugget or two lying around waiting to be pocketed by anyone who'd bother to look, the brothers had figured. Rumors that the mine was haunted, a story they'd heard repeatedly since moving to Lodestone from Los Angeles three months earlier, merely fueled their curiosity about the place.

Gregory and Peter now stood before the rusted metal gate that blocked the narrow entrance to the old Lafferty gold mine. The gate had a faded NO TRESPASSING sign hanging on the bars, secured with a padlock the size of a softball. Like the gate itself, the lock appeared to be rusted solid. Peering into the darkness beyond, the brothers could hear the faint but unmistakable sounds of men calling to one another, and distant clanking noises that sounded like picks and shovels hitting hard stone.

Considering the fact that the Lafferty Mine was shut down over a hundred years ago, and that this gate was still firmly in place, Gregory had to conclude that the ghosts he'd heard the local kids talk about were absolutely real. But rather than being afraid, he found himself excited by the prospect of encountering real ghostly spirits. More than anything, he wanted to get past this gate and see the ghosts for himself, to catch a glimpse of the restless souls that had dwelled within this vast mountain for more than a century.

"This is just too cool," he whispered to his younger, less courageous brother. "I mean, can you imagine what the kids back in L.A. would say if they knew we'd found an actual haunted mine? They'd go nuts!"

"No, they'd say we *were* nuts for staying here," Peter replied, his voice cracking slightly from tension. "Maybe the ghosts don't like trespassers. Maybe they'll get us if we don't get out of here."

"How can a ghost *get* you?" Gregory challenged his sibling. "They're just energy. The most they can do is make noise and maybe throw some things around. But they can't *hurt* you."

Gregory believed himself to be an authority on matters of the supernatural, having recently done a report on the subject for school. Now, hoping to experience firsthand a phenomenon he'd only read about in books, he gripped the barred door and shook it to see if it was secure. The gate moved in his hands, and looking closer, he saw that the frame's ancient moorings had loosened from the rock face to which they'd been anchored.

"Hey, Peter! I bet we can get through here!" Gregory said excitedly as he repositioned the door so that a small space was created between the frame and the rock face. It was just wide enough for a skinny kid his brother's size to squeeze through.

"Hey! What do you kids think you're doing?" a voice suddenly shouted.

Startled, Peter and Gregory spun around to find themselves staring at the ugliest man they'd ever seen. Standing directly behind them, he looked to be about a hundred years old, with a face like a shriveled apple, and thinly matted white hair. His left eye was slammed closed, and the few teeth he had were brown and pointing in every direction. Dressed in a faded flannel shirt, denim overalls, and boots coated with grime, the man stank like week-old roadkill.

The boys both had the exact same immediate reaction. Screaming in terror, they turned and ran. But Peter only got about fifteen feet before he tripped over a rock and went tumbling down the wooded hillside. Gregory caught up with his brother a few seconds later and found him grimacing in pain as he gripped his own right ankle.

"I think I broke my ankle!" Peter cried.

"It's probably just a sprain!" the old man shouted as he stood on the ledge above them. "We should put some ice on it right away to take down the swelling!"

"Stay away from us!" Gregory shouted, still not certain if this disgusting-looking man was friend or foe.

"Hey, I'm not going to hurt you," the old man tried to assure them. "I have a cabin just on the other side of the hill. It's clean and it's got the ice your friend there needs. Now let me help you."

"He's not my friend, he's my brother," Gregory corrected the creepy old man.

"Then it's up to you to take care of him," the old man said. "Now let's get moving before that ankle swells up to the size of a goose egg."

Gregory still didn't know whether or not he could trust this odd-looking stranger. But the pain on his brother's face told him he had little choice. Nodding silently, he didn't protest when the old man came scrambling down the hill with unexpected grace and helped him lift Peter back to his feet.

■ ■ ■ ■

The old man's cabin had a tiny kitchen, complete with a stove, refrigerator, and even a microwave oven. Filling a towel with ice, the man crossed the small living room to where Peter lay on the ratty couch, and pressed the cold towel on the boy's ankle.

"That's a sprain all right, but not a bad one," the old man said. "Now hold this there until I tell you to let go."

"Listen, thanks for helping my brother, Mister, uh . . . ?" Gregory hesitated.

"Dingle," the old man said, flashing the boys a semi-toothless grin. "Professor Thaddeus Dingle. Pleased to make your acquaintance, fellas."

"You're a *professor*?" Peter asked in amazement.

"I used to be," Dingle said. "I used to teach geology at UC San Diego. Gave it up back in '67. Things got too crazy. Too complicated. Traffic. Crowds. Pollution. Who can live like that? So I came up here to get away from it all. So tell me, what were you kids doing sneaking around the old Lafferty Mine?"

"Well, at first we heard that there might still be gold in there," Gregory replied. "We wanted to check it out. And when we got there, we heard the ghosts."

Gregory stopped himself short, realizing how foolish he must sound to this college professor, who probably thought the motion of ghosts was ridiculous. But instead of scoffing at his claim, Professor Dingle appeared genuinely intrigued.

"So, you heard them, too?" he inquired. "What did they sound like?"

"We heard men's voices, and what sounded like picks, shovels, and drills," Gregory reported.

"Yep, those are the ghosts, all right," Professor Dingle said. "They've been banging away inside those tunnels for as long as I've been living up here, and probably for several years before that."

"Why is the mine haunted?" Peter asked, the pain in his ankle having lessened considerably.

"It's quite a story," the old professor said, leaning forward with a glint in his one good eye. "A hundred-some years ago, the Lafferty Mine was one of the most productive in all of California. The gold vein they'd hit was as tall as a pine tree and as long as five football fields. It was the mother lode. But then, on the evening of August 28, 1886, there was an accident in tunnel five.

43

A cave-in. Turns out the folks at the Lafferty Mining Company got greedy, and had cut a few corners when it came to safety. They didn't use enough supports, and as a result, over fifty men were buried alive." The old man shook his head. "Instead of trying to dig the bodies out, the Lafferty people just closed tunnel five permanently and kept on digging everywhere else," he went on after a moment. "But after that, it was just one disaster after another. Equipment failed. Shafts collapsed. Folks said it was the ghosts, the ghosts of the dead miners. They weren't gonna let those greedy sons-of-guns get any more gold. Finally, the Lafferty company just closed the place up. No sense trying to work a cursed gold mine."

"So there *is* still gold in the mountain?" Gregory asked, his eyes lighting up with excitement.

"Tons of it," Dingle replied. "But no one with any sense is gonna go in there trying to dig it out. I told you, the place is haunted, and everyone knows it."

Gregory and Peter exchanged curious looks. Both were thinking the same thing. Ghosts or no ghosts, they had to get into that mine.

■ ■ ■ ■

"I think I can do this," Peter grunted through clenched teeth as he painfully squeezed himself between the gate's loose iron frame and the rock face from which it had partly separated. "There!" Stumbling free, he joined his older brother Gregory who had already squeezed himself past the gate.

It was now five days since their first visit to the old Lafferty Mine and their encounter with the eccentric Professor Dingle. In that time, the swelling in Peter's sprained ankle had gone away, and it was strong enough that he could walk on it without a problem. Having decided ahead of time to revisit the mine and see if they could grab some gold for themselves, this time the brothers arrived with flashlights, small shovels, and buckets in which to carry home the nuggets they hoped to recover.

"All right, Peter. Let's do it," Gregory said, snapping on his flashlight. Leading the way, he started down the ancient tunnel, being careful to avoid tripping over the rotting railroad ties that still held the century-old mine car tracks in place.

They'd only traveled a few hundred feet when Peter grabbed his brother's arm and pulled him to a halt. "Did you hear that?" he gasped.

Indeed, now that they'd stopped moving, Gregory could hear sounds coming from deep within the mine. They were the same sounds they'd heard nearly a week before, the sounds of miners at work.

"Do you th-th-ink those are the d-d-dead miners?" Peter stammered, his eyes wide open.

"I sure hope so," Gregory said, starting to move again. "I've never seen a real live ghost—or should I say, a real *dead* ghost—before!"

Several minutes later, the tunnel jogged sharply to the left. As it did, the tunnel walls began to glow with a warm, amber light. Cautiously moving toward the light source, the brothers found themselves standing near the edge of a sharp precipice. Below them was a huge open crater which had been carved out of the native rock in a series of concentric terraces. The crater was crisscrossed with dozens of catwalks and was illuminated by a string of floodlamps powered by portable electric generators. Everywhere the boys looked they saw men digging away with a combination of old-fashioned picks and shovels and modern-day drilling equipment.

"Those aren't ghosts!" Gregory said to Peter, his voice barely audible over the roar of the mining operation below. "Those are miners!"

"But I thought this mine was closed," Peter said.

"It *is*," Gregory replied. "I bet these guys are crooks! They're probably—"

Just then, a massive hand slammed down on each of the boy's shoulders. Terrified, they were pulled up off their feet by a pair of the biggest, meanest-looking construction workers they'd ever seen.

"What are you kids doing here?" one of them bellowed from beneath his hard hat.

"Um, rock hunting?" Gregory replied meekly.

"Yeah, right," the miner snarled. Then he shoved the boys toward the nearest catwalk. "You're coming with us," he said gruffly. "Mr. Shandler can decide what to do with you."

Gregory had no idea who this Mr. Shandler was, but he had the sickening feeling that he wasn't one of the good guys.

■ ■ ■ ■

Five minutes later, Gregory and Peter found themselves standing before a stern, intelligent-looking man wearing a leather jacket and a hard hat emblazoned with a gold letter "S."

"We caught 'em sneaking around topside, boss," the first worker said. "What should we do with 'em?"

"Who sent you here?" Shandler asked, staring at the trembling boys.

"No one," Gregory replied honestly. "We just heard there was an old gold mine here, and we came to see if we could grab some nuggets for ourselves."

"Didn't you see the warning signs?" Shandler asked sharply. "Is it your habit to trespass on private property?"

"No," Gregory replied. Then, feeling suddenly cocky, he added, "Is it yours?"

Shandler stared at Gregory coldly for several long seconds, then his left eye twitched. "I'm an entrepreneur, a private businessman who seeks out opportunities. Who takes risks. For over a hundred years, this mountain has remained untouched, its resources wasted, all because of some foolish folk legend. I think that's criminal. All I'm doing is fulfilling the American Dream of creating wealth where none existed before."

"You mean *stealing* it, don't you?" Gregory corrected him, his confidence rising by the second.

"And what about the ghosts?" Peter chimed in. "How do you think they're going to feel about you taking their gold?"

"Oh, I don't think they'll miss it," Shandler said, smiling for the first time. "After all, they're dead. Just like you're going to be in four minutes." He turned to the two big miners. "Take these boys into tunnel seven—and eliminate them!"

Just then, the cavern was shaken by a powerful blast as one of the nearby generators exploded in a cloud of smoke and flame. Two more explosions followed. Men screamed. The ground began to tremble, and overhead two catwalks began to collapse, throwing the men crossing them into the mining crater below.

"What's happening?" Shandler shouted.

"It's the ghosts!" Peter screamed. "They've come to stop you once and for all!"

"Run for it!" Gregory screamed, grabbing his brother and dashing away as a chunk of ceiling broke loose causing rocks and stones to rain down on them.

All around them, the boys saw men being crushed beneath boulders and falling into huge cracks in the earth as the whole mountain seemed to start caving in around them. Plunging ahead, somehow managing to sidestep disaster at every turn, Gregory and Peter dashed into the tunnel they'd entered through just as a boulder the size of a barn smashed to the ground behind them.

As they ran, the boys heard screams. Gregory was certain that these were not just the screams of Shandler's men as they faced imminent death, but the wails and moans of souls who'd succumbed to similar fates over a century before. Just as old Professor Dingle had warned them, the spirits of the dead were not about to let their home be disturbed by the greedy.

They were halfway down the tunnel when the mountain shook again and part of the ceiling ahead of them tumbled to the ground in an explosion of stone and dust, blocking the exit. Then the shaking stopped, and the brothers found themselves trapped in silent darkness.

"We gotta get out of here!" Peter cried, clawing at the pile of stones in front of him. "Help! Someone, help us!"

"Calm down!" Gregory ordered. "You'll use up all the oxygen in here!"

"I don't want to die!" Peter whimpered. "I'm only twelve years old! Gregory, I'm scared!"

"We'll be okay," Gregory assured his brother, although he, too, felt tears coming to his eyes. "Maybe if we're careful, we can dig our way out of here."

Working slowly but methodically, the brothers began picking their way through the pile of rocky debris stone by stone. But it soon became clear that the job was far too daunting, that they'd probably suffocate long before they got to the other side. And then, just when Gregory was about to admit defeat, he heard a sharp tapping coming from the other side of the wall.

"There's someone out there!" he cried with excitement. "We're going to be saved!"

A few moments later, a chunk of rock fell forward and a shaft of daylight blazed through the small opening.

"Anyone in there?" a familiar voice asked. The brothers recognized it immediately as Professor Dingle's.

"It's us, Gregory and Peter Ringold!" Gregory shouted. "We're trapped!"

"Hang on, boys!" the professor called. "I've got a shovel here. I'll have you out in just a minute!"

■ ■ ■ ■

When Gregory and Peter returned home later that day, they found the entire town of Lodestone recovering from what they later learned was an area-wide earthquake that had measured 7.2 on the Richter scale. Aftershocks continued throughout the day, keeping everyone's nerves on edge and causing additional damage to many of the town's already weakened structures.

After telling their parents what had happened in agonizing detail, Peter and Gregory were instructed to repeat the story to Chief Quimby, the head of Lodestone's police department. There might still be survivors in the mine, and if nothing else, the bodies of Shandler and his men would have to be removed.

"So I guess the Lafferty Mine wasn't really haunted after all," Gregory concluded after telling the story to Chief Quimby. "There was a rational explanation for everything."

"I'll alert the FBI immediately," the police chief said. "But I have just one more question for you boys. You said you were saved by some guy named Professor Dingle who lived in a cabin up by the mountain?"

"That's right," Peter said. "He said he used to teach geology at UC San Diego."

"Yeah, Gregory agreed. "He moved out here to study the Lafferty Mine. Said he was sure there were ghosts in there."

"That's very interesting," the chief said thoughtfully. "There used to be an old hermit named Dingle living up there. An old geology teacher, as I remember. But he died over ten years ago. After that, his cabin was burned to the ground during a forest fire."

Feeling a sudden, unearthly chill, Gregory turned to his brother in shock. He'd gone to the Lafferty Mine to find a ghost—and maybe he had found one after all.

call me jody

The water was cold. Icy cold. It was the kind of cold that went straight to the bone and made you feel like the finger of Death itself had touched your soul.

Trapped deep beneath the water's dark, murky surface, the young girl struggled desperately for air. Her arms and legs thrashed about madly through the frigid blackness. But there was no escape. Someone—or some *thing*—was pressing on her head, making it impossible for her to rise from the suffocating watery gloom.

As she struggled, her lungs burned, desperate for oxygen. Her body was seized with agonizing cramps, and she felt like her chest was about to explode. She had no choice. She had to open her mouth. To try to breathe. Even if it meant flooding her lungs with the frigid water around her, inviting Death to take her. Soon she would no longer be able to resist.

And so she opened her mouth—and screamed.

■ ■ ■ ■

"I had the drowning dream again last night," Jody Winningham told her parents that morning over breakfast. "It was horrible."

"I know it's scary, sweetheart," her mother said. "But you have to remember, dreams are just dreams. They aren't real."

Jody's mother was dressed for work in a dark gray suit. As a Special Agent for the Federal Bureau of Investigation, she never wore anything but conservative clothing to work.

"But this one *felt* so real," Jody insisted. "It's like I was really there. Like it was really happening. I mean, I could actually *feel* the cold, the water, and when I woke up I was actually shivering."

"You have to remember that dreams are the mind's way of coping with the problems of real life," her father said. Like Jody's mom, he, too, worked for the FBI, and was dressed in a dark gray suit. But unlike her mother, Jody's dad didn't work in the field investigating crimes. Instead, he was a number cruncher who processed crime statistics in a big, computer-filled room. "If you're dreaming that you're drowning, it's probably because you're feeling that you are under pressure at school. Are you having problems with any of your classes?"

"The usual," Jody admitted. "I'm still having a hard time with Spanish. In math and science I'm getting mostly A's and B's, though."

"Maybe we should take you back to Dr. Fields," her mother suggested. "Would you like to start seeing her again?"

Jody thought about all this for a moment. Dr. Lyla Fields was a psychologist she'd seen many years ago when she'd had problems adjusting to a new school. Although her memories of that period were blurry, Jody did remember that Dr. Fields had been a very warm, friendly woman whom Jody could talk to openly without fear of being judged. If Dr. Fields could help her get rid of her recurring nightmares, that would be wonderful. But at the same time Jody didn't want to be known as a kid who needed a shrink. If she did decide to see Dr. Fields, she'd better not tell any of her classmates.

"Let's wait and see," Jody finally replied. "Maybe the dreams will go away by themselves."

"Let's hope so," her mother said, then threw her husband a worried look that Jody found strangely unsettling.

■ ■ ■ ■

"I'm thinking of cutting my hair," Jody said to her friend Tina Gorsky as they both stood in front of the mirror in the girls' rest room. "Maybe even coloring it blond instead of this yucky dull brown color. What do you think?"

"I like your hair the way it is," Tina replied as she brushed out her own brown curls. "Why mess with a good thing?"

"I don't know," Jody said uncomfortably, pulling her hair back to reveal more of her face. "This just doesn't feel right anymore. Y'all know what I mean?"

"*Y'all?*" Tina exclaimed, raising her eyebrows. "Why the Southern accent all of a sudden?"

Jody was as dumbfounded as her friend. The Southern inflection had somehow felt as natural to her as, well, breathing. She was trying to come up with a believable response when she turned back to the mirror and was shocked to see someone else's face staring back! It was the face of a younger girl—perhaps six years old—with short, blond hair. Startled, Jody screamed.

"What is it?" Tina asked urgently. "What's wrong, Jody?"

"I—I've seen that girl," Jody stammered, pointing to the mirror. But as she did, the mysterious girl vanished.

"Of course you have," Tina replied nervously. "That's you."

Not knowing what to say, Jody turned and hurried from the rest room. She couldn't tell her friend what had happened, because the truth was, she didn't even know herself. All she knew was that it felt like another presence had invaded her body just before the vision had appeared in the mirror. She wanted to resist it. To fight it off. But how could she when she didn't even know where her true self ended and this new entity began?

■ ■ ■ ■

The cold water enveloped her like a frigid blanket. The girl clawed her way to the surface, but she was being dragged deeper and deeper by a force she did not understand.

And then, through the murky blackness, she heard a woman's voice. Someone was shouting. Someone was calling her name. "Emma!" the voice cried. "Emma!"

■ ■ ■ ■

"The girl's name is Emma Broyles," Jody told her parents that morning.

"Who is Emma Broyles?" her dad asked. He had been extremely tense and anxious ever since Jody had come home late from school two days earlier with her hair cut really short and dyed blond.

"The girl in my dream," Jody replied. "The girl who's drowning. The last time I had the dream, I heard someone call her first name, and all of a sudden I knew that her full name was Emma Broyles."

"But I thought *you* were the one drowning in the dream," her mother said as she sat down in the chair beside her daughter. Like her husband, Jody's mom had not been at all happy with her daughter's new look and still had a difficult time looking straight at her.

"So did I, but it's not me," Jody said, still trying to make sense of it all herself. "I mean, the girl in the dream is Emma Broyles, only I'm seeing her death through *her* eyes."

"This is starting to sound like one of those *Weird World* shows," her mother said with a nervous laugh, referring to a popular TV program that focused on ghosts, ESP, UFOs, and other paranormal phenomena.

"I seriously think it's time you saw Dr. Fields," her father said grimly. "These kinds of dreams can't be healthy. In fact, they could be very—"

"No, I don't want to see her," Jody replied firmly. "I want to find out more about Emma Broyles. Maybe there's something about her death at the library."

"You'd just be wasting your time," her father said sternly. "Emma Broyles is probably just a name you heard on the news or read in a book."

"Maybe you're right, Dad," Jody said with a heavy sigh as she stood up from the table. "But I've got to find out one way or the other."

As she left the room, Jody couldn't help noticing how upset her parents looked. Maybe she should have asked them before she cut and dyed her hair. But she would have done it anyway—it was as if she *had* to. Just like she *had* to discover the truth about Emma Broyles.

■　■　■　■

Jody's junior high school had an excellent student library. With the help of Ms. Lardner, the young school librarian, she learned how to access the library's extensive collection of local newspapers, all of which had been converted to CD-ROM.

"All you have to do is enter a key word or phrase, such as 'bank robberies,' and every article that has appeared on that topic in the last twenty-five years will be listed," Ms. Lardner explained. "Then just use the mouse to click on the story you want. Just what topic are you looking for?"

"It's kind of personal," Jody replied. "But thanks anyway."

"My pleasure," Ms. Lardner said with a smile. "Always happy to help an inquisitive student."

After Ms. Lardner had returned to the front desk, Jody sat down at the keyboard and typed the words *drowning accidents* and then *Emma Broyles*. She didn't have to wait long for the results to appear. Two stories came up, each written just a day apart, eight years earlier. Grabbing the mouse, Jody called up the first story, and then began to read the front-page article.

■　■　■　■

"Emma Broyles was real," Jody announced triumphantly later that evening. She slid photocopies of both newspaper articles across the table to where her parents sat. Their faces held grim, almost sickly expressions. "She was found drowned up at Lake Plymouth eight years ago. She was six years old then, which would make her my age now—if she'd survived. But not only did Emma die, so did her parents. They were murdered two days earlier in their home in Atlanta, Georgia."

Her parents didn't even bother to look at the stories. Instead, they turned directly to their daughter and regarded her with stern looks on their faces.

"This has nothing to do with you," her father stated.

"We want you to forget about this, Jody," her mother insisted. She took the articles and folded them in half. "And we want you to start seeing Dr. Fields. In fact, we made an appointment for you to see her tomorrow afternoon right after school, okay?"

"No!" Jody shouted, jumping to her feet. "There's nothing Dr. Fields can do. For some reason, Emma's spirit has chosen me. I think she wants me to find the person who murdered her, and I don't want to let her down!"

"*Murdered?*" her mother gasped in surprise. "Who says she was murdered? These stories only say she was drowned. It was an accident, pure and simple."

"I believe Emma was *killed* deliberately," Jody insisted. "And I can't believe that as FBI agents you're not the least bit interested in that." She paused to collect her thoughts. "Please, Mom, Dad," she went on with pleading eyes. "I need to find out how Emma died. I need you to take me up to Lake Plymouth."

"I'm sorry," her father said, shaking his head. "This fantasy of yours is getting out of control. You're not going up there. Don't even think about it."

"You're going to see Dr. Fields tomorrow, and that's final," her mother said flatly. "And I don't ever want to hear another word about Emma Broyles, understand?"

Jody just stared back in angry silence. As far as she was concerned, her parents could protest all they wanted, but somehow she was going to go to Lake Plymouth, even if it was the last thing she ever did.

■ ■ ■ ■

"I really appreciate this, Steve," Jody told Tina Gorsky's older brother as they took Highway 8 into the Redstone Mountains.

"Hey, no problem," Steve replied, his fingers tapping the steering wheel to the music on the radio. "I like to get out of the city every now and then. Breathe the fresh mountain air."

Jody hadn't had any trouble convincing Tina and Steve to take her up to a beautiful place like Lake Plymouth for the day, although she never told them exactly *why* she wanted to go. How could she explain that she was trying to learn more about a drowned girl who had taken over her dreams?

Just under two hours after leaving the city, the trio stopped off a narrow paved road that ran along the lake. Jody stepped out of the car and gazed out over the smooth, dark blue waters. In the distance, a series of dark, jagged peaks stood like silent sentinels, forever guarding the lake and its terrible secrets.

"This is where I died," Jody whispered.

"What do you mean, *you* died?" Tina asked. "You're talking like a crazy person!"

Ignoring her friend's question, Jody moved dreamlike toward the edge of the placid waters. As she did, Steve turned to his sister and shot her a "What's-going-on-here?" look.

"I was running away," Jody went on, addressing neither Tina nor her brother directly. "Someone was chasing me, but I was too small and couldn't run fast enough to get away."

60

Suddenly Jody whipped around, her eyes wide with terror. "No!" she screamed. "Stay away! Let me go!"

"Jody, what's wrong?" Tina shouted. "You're scaring me!"

But Jody had already spun around and was running madly along the edge of the lake, screaming like a little girl.

"Stop her!" Tina shouted as she and her brother dashed after her friend.

Jody could barely breathe. The thin mountain air was making her lungs burn as she gasped, trying to fill them with oxygen. Still fleeing her unseen pursuer, she stumbled out into the water. She'd only taken a few steps when she lost her balance, fell forward, and plunged into the icy depths.

The frigid waters enveloped her, held her fast, and pulled her down. She thrashed her arms and legs madly as raw panic overtook her and left her completely disoriented. Her clothes and jacket, now laden with water, became impossibly heavy, their weight pulling her farther and farther away from the light above her.

And then, over the deafening sounds of her heart pounding in her ears, she heard a voice cry, "Jody! Jody!" She felt something grip her upraised hand, and suddenly she was crashing back up through the surface, gulping cold, fresh air. She caught a fleeting glimpse of her father, his face streaked with water, before she closed her eyes and fell back into his strong, steady arms.

■ ■ ■ ■

"We tried to hide the truth from you as long as we could," Jody's mother said as the three of them drove back toward home. They'd found out from Tina and Steve's parents where the kids

61

had gone and had raced up to the lake as soon as they could. "It was for your own protection."

"But the little girl who died, Emma Broyles . . . " Jody began softly, her thoughts still confused even a full hour after her father had pulled her from the icy lake. "She was—"

"She *didn't* die," her father interrupted, his eyes fixed firmly on the road ahead. "We've been trying to tell you, honey. You *are* Emma Broyles."

"Emma's parents—*your* parents—were lawyers, and they did some legal work for organized crime figures awhile ago in Atlanta," her mother explained. "While working on a case, they came across information they shouldn't have, and the Mob had them killed. You were in the house at the time, and the killer thought you might be able to identify him."

"He kidnapped you in Atlanta," her father said, jumping in to continue the story. "Then he brought you all the way up here hoping that, being so far away from home, no one would be able to identify your body."

"My *body?*" Jody repeated, her voice shaking.

"He tried to drown you in the lake," her father said, his voice straining with emotion. "And he might have succeeded, but some hikers found your body and were able to revive you with CPR."

"After you were identified as the Broyles's daughter, we were assigned to the case," her mother said, holding her daughter tightly. "We found you suffering from a severe case of traumatic amnesia. You had no memory of who you were. You could barely speak."

"Anyway, we both fell instantly in love with you," her father said with a warm smile. "And since we'd already been married for ten years and hadn't been able to have a child, we decided to adopt you."

"With the help of Dr. Fields, we were able to get you speaking again," her mother went on. "Using hypnosis, she was able to supply you with partial memories to replace those you'd lost. And luckily your blond hair naturally turned darker as you grew older, so it was easy for us to pretend you were actually someone else."

"You know," her father noted with a laugh. "We've repeated these stories about your childhood so often, it's like they've become our memories, too!"

Jody looked from one parent to the other. "So, you aren't my real parents?" she asked.

"Not your biological ones," her mother replied.

"Dr. Fields warned us that your old memories might start resurfacing at some point," her dad said. "We just weren't sure exactly when."

"The hit man, the guy who tried to kill me—whatever happened to him?" Jody asked fearfully.

"We never caught him," her father admitted. "We planted those stories you found in the local paper to make it look like you'd drowned, but as far as we know, he's still out there."

Jody shuddered to think what might happen if the Mob assassin discovered that she was still alive, that she still might be able to identify him. Even though eight whole years had passed, she still could wind up floating at the bottom of the lake's dark depths after all.

"The killer, what did he look like?" Jody asked.

"We never got a complete description," her dad replied. "Supposedly, he was a master of disguise. All we knew for sure was that he had a tattoo of a broken heart on his left forearm."

"Now that you know the truth, I guess you have to make a choice," her mother said softly. "Do you want to be Jody Winningham or Emma Broyles?"

Jody looked at her mother and father, the only two parents she'd really ever known. These were the people who'd saved her from the brink of death, not just once, but twice. They were the ones who had given her a home, who had given her love. The choice was simple.

"Mom, Dad," she said, tears in her eyes. "Call me Jody."

■ ■ ■ ■

Jody was sitting in a far corner of the school library preparing for her American history exam when Ms. Lardner appeared behind her.

"Hi, Jody," she said with a warm smile. "Did you ever find what you were looking for?"

"As a matter of fact, I did," Jody replied. "It took a while, but I found *exactly* what I was looking for."

"You and I both," the librarian said with a wicked smile. "It took me a long time, but I finally found exactly what *I've* been looking for, too."

Before Jody could ask Ms. Lardner what she was talking about, she felt a powerful arm lock around her throat. Looking down, she was terrified to see—on the woman's exposed, muscular forearm—a tattoo in the shape of a broken heart.

number one fan

rom The Journal of Ben Gutierrez:
September 8, 1997:

I'm really upset. *Crazed* might be a better word. I just found out that Don Ludlum has just been elected president of the Ken Corbin Fan Club. That was supposed to be *my* job. I earned it. I've been Ken Corbin's number one fan ever since his first CD, *Pavement Narrows*, came out five years ago. I know everything there is to know about Ken Corbin. I know that he was born in Sheboygan, Wisconsin, on December 22, 1964. I know his parents were killed in a car crash when he was five years old. And I know he hates to have his picture taken. In fact, as far as I know, there *are* no pictures of Ken Corbin anywhere. There are paintings and drawings, but no photographs.

There are many theories as to why you can't find a photograph of Ken Corbin to save your life. Some people say he's just really, really shy. Others say that he believes photography snatches away part of your soul, something he'd like to avoid. Then there's the theory that there really is no Ken Corbin, that he's just a character made up by a bunch of studio musicians.

But my favorite theory is that Ken was banged up real bad in the same car wreck that killed his parents, and now he's really, really ugly. So ugly that he's afraid his fans would be terrified if they ever saw his real face. He's like this horrible monster—with a great voice. I think that's really cool.

Anyway, if I'm such an expert on Ken Corbin, why did Don get the president's job instead of me? Because Don's dad manages Pier Music in the South Park Mall, and he can get everyone a 10 percent discount there, that's why! It was nothing but pure bribery! And I refuse to stand for it! I'm going to have Don's job if it's the last thing I do!

■ ■ ■ ■

September 15, 1997:

I've complained to all twenty members of our club about how unfairly I've been treated, but nothing has changed. Don is still president, and I'm still just another lowly club member. But this is going to change very soon.

You see, *my* dad installs air conditioning systems, and just yesterday he was doing some duct work in one of the local recording studios when he overheard some guys saying that Ken Corbin was coming to town next week to cut some tracks for his next CD. Can you believe that? *The* Ken Corbin, right here in Evanston, Illinois!

Obviously, the first thing I thought was, Wow, I've got to meet the guy! And then I had another, even better idea. I'm going to take his picture! Can you just imagine that? Me, having the only known photo of the greatest singer-songwriter of the entire 1990s!

I don't care *how* ugly he is. When I bring that picture to our club meeting, I'll be a hero, and Don Ludlum will be nothing but history.

■ ■ ■ ■

September 20th, 1997:

My quest to get a picture of Ken Corbin is right on schedule. Right after I wrote my last journal entry, I called up the studio where my dad said Ken Corbin was going to record his CD. After giving me the runaround for about fifteen minutes, they finally said that my dad had heard wrong, that Ken Corbin wasn't even coming to Evanston, that he was going to record his next CD in London.

I knew they were lying, of course. If they weren't talking to Ken Corbin's people, how could they know about London? The way I figured it, they couldn't admit that Ken Corbin was going to be there or the place would be overrun with idiot fans wanting his autograph and nosy reporters trying to take his picture like a bunch of fools.

So I called up all the hotels within five miles of the studio to see if any of them had a reservation in Ken Corbin's name. Just as I expected, everyone said no. Especially the Park Plaza Hotel. They *really* said no. Like fifteen times. And then they told me never to call there again. Which told me that this was where Ken Corbin would be staying.

So now I'm ready to make my move. In a few more days, I should have the answer to one of the greatest mysteries of the era: Just what the heck does Ken Corbin *really* look like?

■ ■ ■ ■

September 25th, 1997:

I've spent the last week hanging out at the Park Plaza Hotel every day after school. I've been telling the people there that I'm doing a report on the hotel itself for my English class, and they've been happy to talk to me.

So far I've made friends with several of the housekeepers, including Maria Lamm, who works on the top floor. She's promised to help me get into Ken's suite once he's checked in. In return for her help, I've promised to tutor Maria's two kids in English for a month. If I get this interview, the price will be worth it.

■ ■ ■ ■

October 30, 1997:

I realize I haven't written in a while, but things have been kind of, well, strange lately. Here's what happened:

Just after 7:00 on Friday evening, I got a call from Maria Lamm saying that Ken Corbin and his people had just checked in. I had already told my folks I was spending the night at my friend Benny's house, so there was no problem with me leaving at that hour. I grabbed my pocket-sized camera and, instead of going to Benny's, I rode my bike straight to the Park Plaza Hotel, naturally.

70

When I got there, Maria told me that Ken had already left. I figured he was going to the studio to record his tracks. (All the music magazines said that Ken liked to work at night.) I asked Maria for permission to wait until Ken came back, and she said there was no problem. I was even allowed to rest in a small storage area that had been turned into a bunk room where some of the housekeepers rested between shifts.

And there I sat, waiting for Ken Corbin to come back to the hotel. I sat and I sat, and by 11:30 I was so sleepy that I had to lie down. I must have fallen asleep, because the next time I opened my eyes and looked at my watch, it was 8:00 in the morning! I'd slept through the entire night!

Climbing out of the cot, I found Maria just checking in for her day's work. I told her what happened and asked if there was any way she could get me up to the hotel's top floor.

"I can get you up there, but the security people will probably catch you and throw you out," she warned me.

"Not if I hide," I said slyly, eyeing the large wheeled laundry cart that sat against the nearby wall.

With my tape recorder in hand, I climbed into the cart, then crouched down as Maria threw several old sheets on top of me. She then wheeled me into the nearby service elevator which whisked us both up to the top of the building.

"I'm just here to change the sheets," Maria told the bodyguard seconds after she stepped off the elevator. I heard the man grunt his approval, then we rolled down the hall.

"Housekeeping!" Maria called after lightly knocking on the door. There was no answer. I then heard the jingle of keys and five seconds later we were in Ken Corbin's room.

As soon as Maria shut the door, I scrambled out of the cart, stretched out my aching limbs, and looked around. This was a magnificent three-room suite—the best in the city, so I'd been

71

told—decorated with gorgeous antiques. It was just the kind of room a president, a millionaire, or a rock star would be expected to stay in.

Maria looked in each of the two bedrooms, then turned back to me and shrugged. "He's not here," she said, clearly puzzled. "I'm going to change the sheets. You can stay here if you want."

"Thanks," I said gratefully, then flopped down on the plush velvet-covered couch. Twenty minutes later, Maria had finished her job and was preparing to leave.

"You're going to stay here and wait?" she asked.

"If I can," I replied hopefully, nervously fingering the camera tucked in my front pocket.

"Good luck," Maria said. "And, remember, if anyone asks how you got in here—"

"I never saw you before in my life," I replied.

Maria smiled, flashed me a thumbs up, then exited the room with her laundry cart.

When she was gone I gave a deep sigh, then decided to check out the place to see if I could find any souvenirs I could snatch for my collection. The living area appeared to be completely unlived-in. There wasn't a thing here that the hotel hadn't provided. So I moved into the master suite, hoping to find some of Ken's personal items. There I saw something that caught me completely by surprise. It was a long wooden box set atop two wooden saw horses. Although the curtains were drawn over the windows and the room was dark, I recognized it as the kind of box in which technicians haul around speakers or electrical equipment. What was it doing here in Ken's bedroom?

Totally curious, I approached the box to check it out. I slowly ran my hand over its rough wooden surface, and as I did, a strange electric tingling danced through my fingers. I looked down to see if maybe some machine inside could be plugged into the wall, but I saw no electrical cord.

It was then that I noticed the lid was hinged. There was no clasp or lock holding it in place. Desperate to see what was inside, I grabbed the lid and raised it.

Instantly, I was hit with a stench so foul I thought I was going to vomit right then and there. My eyes watered and I nearly choked on the wretched fumes.

As my vision cleared, I saw myself staring down at something I never in a million years expected to be there. Thin, pale, with sunken cheeks framed by long black hair, the face was one I'd seen in countless paintings, line drawings, and charcoal sketches. It was the face of Ken Corbin.

I found myself in total shock. First, there was the fact that he looked just like his pictures, which was the last thing I'd expected. I mean, I'd been led to believe that he had the face of some weird, deformed monster, which he obviously didn't. The other thing that got me was the fact *he wasn't breathing*. From the looks of things, this man—my hero—was *dead*!

"Somebody killed Ken Corbin!" I cried, believing at this moment that someone had murdered the superstar and placed his body in this box for a secret burial.

But no sooner had I said this than the man's eyes snapped open, he reached up with his right hand and grabbed me by the throat in a grip so strong I was sure he was going to crush my windpipe.

"Who let you in here?" Ken snarled.

"M-m-my name is Ben Gutierrez, and I'm your number one fan," I managed to stammer out. "I was hoping you'd let me take your picture." As I spoke, I realized how pathetic I sounded.

"No one takes my picture!" the thing called Ken Corbin hissed. "You see, it can't be done!"

73

With that, he gave a broad, almost comical smile, and I suddenly realized why this singer was so secretive, why he always worked at night, and why he never, ever let himself be photographed. The truth was, his image couldn't register on film. Just like it couldn't reflect in a mirror. For as the long, sharp fangs protruding from his upper gums confirmed, Ken Corbin was a vampire.

"Still, you shouldn't go away empty-handed," Ken said, his breath smelling like the bottom of an ancient grave. "As my number one fan, you should have something to remember me by."

With that, he prepared to plunge his fangs into my neck.

■ ■ ■ ■

April 8, 2057:

This will serve as a belated postscript to my original journal. Reading over my old childhood notes, I realize that I've left many questions unanswered. I will try to address them as best I can.

First, I obviously never did get my picture of Ken Corbin. But I did visit him two more times while he was in town—all at his invitation—and I soon completely forgot about why I'd come to his hotel in the first place.

Just like I forgot about my desire to be president of the Ken Corbin Fan Club, and going back to school, for that matter.

Now, as one of the undead, I find I have very few mortal desires at all. Feeling strangely powerful, yet lacking any kind of direction, I decided to do the only thing that now made sense. I joined Ken Corbin's "band" and dedicated myself to his service.

Which is where I remain to this very day. Of course, I don't call Ken Corbin by that name anymore. Over the years, he's changed his name to "Jeff Bayless," "Todd Temkin," and, most recently, "Quinn Farquar." Regardless of what name he may use during any particular decade, I still find him fascinating—a man over two hundred centuries old still driving the kids wild.

Anyway, the next time a reclusive superstar comes to town, take a close look at his backup singers. If you see a dark-haired boy who looks like he belongs in junior high school, that might be me. Come up to my hotel room, and I'll tell you all about what it's like to travel with a rock star.

Just don't try to take my picture.

body donor

This man was not Brendan Chung. Granted, he looked just like Nina's widowed father. He talked just like him. He even wore the same clothes and had the same light brown eyes. But as soon as the man walked into the Chungs' apartment here on level four of the Martian mining and research colony known as New Los Angeles, Nina knew that something was wrong.

What tipped her off was what he did when he first came home from work at the colony's Transmatter Operations Center. Ever since Nina could remember, even when they were living back on Earth, her dad would call, "Nina! I'm home!" as soon as he walked through the front door. But tonight there was only silence. When Nina emerged from her bedroom to see what was wrong, she found her father standing by the door, looking around almost as if he were lost.

"Dad, are you all right?" she asked, concerned.

"Huh?" her father replied, turning to her with a complete look of shock on his face. It was as if he hadn't expected her to be there.

"Have a hard day?" Nina asked. "You don't look so good."

"Me? No, no, I'm fine," the man said haltingly, a strange, faraway expression in his eyes.

Nina looked at him carefully. He seemed distant, almost nervous. "Listen, Dad," she said. "Why don't you sit down and I'll make us dinner. How about some soup?"

"Soup? Yes, soup would be good," her father responded. "Onion, if you have it."

Nina nearly stopped in her tracks. *Onion soup?* Her father disliked onion soup so much that they hadn't even bothered to program it into their kitchen computer.

"Um, I don't think we have any onion soup," Nina said, watching the man closely. "Would *chicken* soup be okay? I think we might have some of that."

"Of course," her father said with a smile. "I'd like that. Thank you, daughter."

Nina flinched again. Never in her life had her father ever referred to her as "daughter." It was either "Nina," "sweetheart," or even "kid." But never the D-word.

All during their meal, Nina kept a close eye on the man claiming to be her father, Brendan Chung. Something was definitely wrong. For one thing, he noisily slurped his soup, which he never had done before. He tucked his napkin under his chin, when in the past he'd always laid it across his lap. But most frightening of all, he ate with his right hand. Nina knew for a fact that her father was *left*-handed.

There was only one conclusion Nina could come to. This man might look like her father, and talk like her father, but he was *not* her father.

Terrified that something awful had happened to her *real* dad, Nina wanted to confront this impostor here and now and demand the truth. But she resisted the urge, knowing that by revealing her suspicions, she might make herself the next target of whatever mysterious forces had decided to make off with her real dad. So she kept quiet, and resolved to find out what had happened to the *real* Brendan Chung.

■ ■ ■ ■

The next morning, after watching her so-called "father" eat an omelet—the real Brendan Chung didn't even eat eggs—Nina followed the man as he walked the four blocks through the colony's underground tunnels to work.

She arrived at the Transmatter Operations Center in New L.A.'s warehousing complex ten minutes later. Access to this part of the colony was restricted to people with high-level security clearance. To enter, you had to have your eyes scanned by a special machine, which would then compare the blood vessel patterns on the back of your retina with the patterns already on file with the center's central computer. Fortunately, Nina had often accompanied her dad to work when she didn't have classes, so she was registered and had no trouble passing the eyeball-scan.

As she walked through the heavy steel doors that led to the control center, she realized something. Whoever the impostor was, he had to have duplicated her real father's retina patterns to get in here!

79

Wow, she thought. Someone actually made an exact copy of the back of my dad's eyeballs! This guy is good!

The Transmatter Operations Center was a large, crescent-shaped room. In it, more than a dozen technicians in light blue lab coats operated a large, complex instrument that reduced items such as food, building materials, and furniture into electronic impulses and recorded them onto 12-inch computer discs. These lightweight discs could then be transported between Earth, Mars, and the other inhabited planets of the solar system far more efficiently than if they were in the normal solid state.

In fact, it was the invention of the Transmatter in 2031 that made the human colonization of outer space even possible, since it lowered transportation costs enormously. For example, all the materials needed to build New Los Angeles were carried to Mars aboard a single lightweight spacecraft, instead of taking the fleet of ships that would have been required before the Transmatter was invented.

What still puzzled scientists, however, was how to record people and other living things without killing them. So far, researchers had been able to reduce and record a few small primates, but the animals always died upon re-materialization. As a result, people and animals still had to travel between worlds the old-fashioned way, aboard huge, resource-guzzling rocket ships.

Now, trying to appear nonchalant, Nina approached Lois Kane, a young woman she'd met on her earlier visits who was responsible for making sure that the Transmatter's programming stayed free of glitches. Even the slightest error, according to her *real* father, could cause an object to be improperly integrated and come out looking like nothing but a formless pile of goo.

"Hi, Lois," Nina said as casually as she could. "How are things going?"

"Oh, hello, Nina," Lois said, looking up from her flat-screen computer display. "Everything's great. You here with your dad?"

"Look, I was wondering, has anything strange been happening around here lately?" Nina replied, not answering the question. "My dad hasn't been acting like himself, and I was thinking maybe he's worried about something going on here at the center."

"Oh, he's probably upset about what happened to Bryan Gridley," Lois said in a hushed voice. "We all are."

"What happened?" Nina asked, her heart suddenly missing a beat. She knew Bryan Gridley only by name. He was one of her father's top programmers.

"He got some bad news from his doctor a few weeks ago," Lois said sadly. "Cancer. A very rare form. Incurable even with gene therapy."

"That's awful," Nina gasped. For decades, cancer—once the most dreaded of diseases—had been as easy to cure as a broken bone. But every once in a while a new variety appeared that resisted even the most powerful medical treatments. Apparently Bryan Gridley had been the victim of just such a superform.

It made sense to Nina that her father might become sullen and distant when one of his closest associates became terminally ill—but this bad news still didn't explain his sudden love of onion soup, or his overnight preference for using his right hand. No, something else was going on here besides the imminent death of one of his co-workers. Something much more sinister was happening.

"No one has seen Bryan for days," Lois went on. "He's probably at home trying to get his affairs in order. But his wife's still here."

She pointed across the room to Selma Gridley, a systems technician. The young, dark-haired woman was sitting at one of the computer control consoles reviewing a report. Nina was about to go to her and express her sympathies when the woman looked up toward a nearby doorway. Nina's father was standing there, signaling Selma to follow him. Giving a quick look around as if to see if anyone was watching, Selma nervously stood and hurried to join Brendan Chung in the adjacent room. Selma's odd behavior immediately sent Nina's suspicions into high gear.

Terrified of what would happen to her if she was caught snooping, Nina quickly followed them, and what she saw next nearly made her heart stop cold. Selma Gridley and her "dad" were standing in the otherwise deserted corridor—and they had their arms around each other!

He must be comforting her, Nina thought, desperate to excuse the behavior of the man she still regarded as her father. He must be trying to make her feel better after what's been happening to her husband.

But even as Nina watched, she heard Selma Gridley laugh. Then Nina's "father" leaned down and *kissed* Selma smack-dab on the lips!

This was too much for Nina to handle.

Feeling sick to her stomach, she turned away and ran as quickly as she could out of the Transmatter Operations Center. She felt like her entire world was falling apart, like everything she'd come to know and trust was proving to be a lie. How could she possibly live another second with this impostor, for she knew her real father would never have an affair with another man's wife!

If only Mom was still alive, Nina thought sadly. Then I could go back to Earth and live with her. But ever since her mother had died in that awful airplane crash two years ago, Nina had had no choice but to live with her father here on Mars. Only this man *wasn't* her father—she was sure of it. Now the only question was how could she prove such a wild accusation? She definitely had to have a plan.

■ ■ ■ ■

"Nina, I'm going over to Selma Gridley's to go over some new program specs she's been working on," the man who claimed to be her father said, poking his head into her bedroom and offering her an uncomfortable smile.

Nina, who was sitting at her desk, looked up. "Before you go, can you sign this for me?" she asked, holding up a slip of paper. "It's a field trip permission form from school. We're going out to explore the caves at—"

"Fine," her "father" said, cutting her off. He grabbed the slip, quickly signed his name in the appropriate space, then handed it back. "I'll see you later." With that, her "dad" was out the door.

Nina shook her head. Boy, Bryan Gridley isn't even dead yet, and this impostor is already going after his wife! she thought in amazement. Then she looked at the permission slip her so-called father had just signed, and her stomach sank right down to the soles of her feet. The signature was nothing at all like her real dad's.

This clinches it, she thought, tears welling up in her eyes. This man is definitely *not* my dad! So who is he? And what does he want with Selma Gridley?

Nina guessed that the answer to this mystery might lie with Selma's husband, Bryan. Having never even met the man, Nina switched on her home computer and called up his file on the colony's resident database. According to the record that appeared on the screen, Bryan was thirty years old, five-foot-ten inches tall, weighed 169 pounds, and had blond hair and green eyes. But what really drew Nina's eyes to the screen was Bryan Gridley's sample signature.

There was something odd about the way the man wrote the "B" in "Bryan" that caught Nina's attention. It was very wide and way out of scale with the rest of the letters. In fact, it was identical to the "B" in the word "Brendan" her "dad" had just signed on her permission slip. Also, the loop-de-loop in the "d" of "Brendan" was just like the "d" in "Gridley."

These features, plus the degree of slant and the overall shape of the letters in both signatures, led Nina to a chilling conclusion: the man posing as her father was, in fact, none other than Bryan Gridley.

But how was that possible? Although both men were approximately the same height and weight, Gridley looked nothing at all like her dad. Among other things, Gridley was a Caucasian, whereas the Chungs were of Asian descent. All the plastic surgery in the world couldn't change a person *that* much! Plus her so-called father had passed the Transmatter Operation Center's retina exam, and there was no way to duplicate another person's appearance all the way down to the blood vessels in his eyes. And besides, why go through all the trouble of making yourself look like someone else when you've been told you're going to die soon, anyway? Unless Gridley wasn't dying after all!

Staring at the photo of Bryan Gridley now staring back at her from her computer screen, an answer began to slowly form in Nina's mind. When it finally came together, she wanted to scream at the top of her lungs. The plot was as brilliant as it was frightening, as amazing as it was diabolical. But above all,

Nina realized that if she was to have any hope of ever seeing her real father in the flesh again, she was going to have to move fast —*very fast*.

■ ■ ■ ■

"Nina, what are you doing here?" the man pretending to be Brendan Chung asked angrily when he opened the door of the Gridleys' apartment to see Nina standing in the corridor beyond.

"I need to talk to you and Mrs. Gridley," Nina replied nervously. "It's very important."

The man ushered her into the small but neatly maintained apartment, then shut the door behind him. Selma Gridley was sitting on the living room couch. Two glasses of wine sat at the coffee table in front of her.

"Well?" her so-called father demanded. "What's this all about, daughter?"

"I know you're not my father," Nina stated flatly. "I know that you're an imposter."

"Well, Nina, you're obviously very upset about something, but I—"

But Nina immediately cut him off. "You've found a way to record living matter," she stated. "You somehow got my father to go into the Transmatter, then recorded him on a disc." She turned to Selma. "Then your husband stepped in and you did the same thing to him."

"That's ridiculous," Selma said with a laugh. "Even if we *could* record living matter, why would I put your father and my husband on a disc?"

"To save your husband's life," Nina said with just a hint of sadness in her voice. "He was dying of cancer, and since

85

his body was doomed, you needed a new one. That's why you chose my dad as your *body donor*. He's about the same size as your husband."

"Chose him for *what*?" Selma cried, sounding more defensive than confused.

"A brain transplant," Nina replied. "You developed a program that allowed you to electronically transfer Bryan's brain into my father's body. Just like an old-time electronic edit. Then, when you reassembled them, the man who came out had not my father's, but your husband's mind! That's why he suddenly likes onion soup, calls me 'daughter,' and writes with his right hand!"

The man in her father's body turned to Selma Gridley. "I told you we'd never pull this off."

"Don't panic, Bryan," Selma said, calmly reaching into a drawer inside her coffee table. "She can't prove anything. Not if she has no mouth to speak with."

Nina turned to run. But before she could get away, Selma whipped out a small pistol-like device. It was a personal tranquilizer, what people now used for home protection ever since old-fashioned handguns had been outlawed.

"Say nightie-night, Nina," Selma said with a twisted grin.

■ ■ ■ ■

Nina awoke, dazed and disoriented, to find herself lying on a clear plastic floor. Below her were rows of hundreds of tiny lights. The ceiling was covered with a similar material, whereas the curved walls were all shiny black. Having seen this place many times before from the outside, Nina recognized it immediately. It was the Transmatter Chamber.

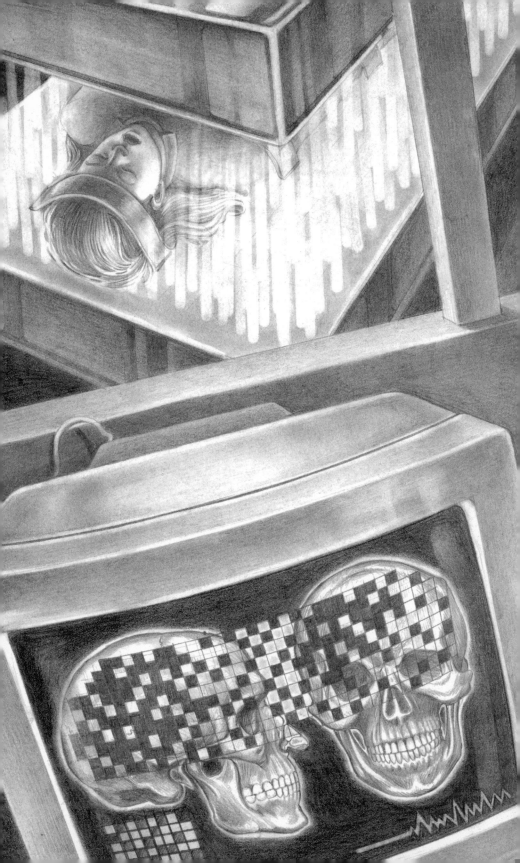

They're going to de-materialize me! she realized in horror. They're going to use this machine to break my body down into trillions of tiny electronic bits. I'll be nothing but a binary code on some computer disc!

Strapped down and struggling to move, Nina managed to see through the thick, clear plastic window of the control room beyond. Selma and Bryan Gridley—he still in her father's body—were preparing the operation.

"You can't do this!" Nina screamed. "It's murder!"

She saw Selma lean forward and flip on the intercom switch. "Don't worry, my dear, it'll be over before you know it," the woman said with a sneer. "You won't feel a thing. And you won't say a thing ever again."

"I won't tell anyone what you did, I promise," Nina said tearfully. "Just let me out of here. Please!"

"Too late, Nina," said Bryan Gridley, speaking in her father's voice. "Besides, Selma and I plan to leave New Los Angeles and return to Earth as soon as possible. You'd only get in the way."

"You're going to sell this process, aren't you?" Nina asked, desperately stalling for time. "You think you'll get rich by selling the secret for recording living matter."

"No, we don't *think* that," Selma replied calmly. "We *know* it for a fact. We've already gotten offers worth over one hundred million dollars, and that's just for starters. In a way, we have your father here to thank for that."

"What do you mean?" Nina asked.

"Brendan made a key breakthrough two months ago," Bryan explained. "That's the main reason why I chose him as my body donor. This way I got a healthy body to live in, and at the same time I eliminated my research competition."

"Now we can keep the secret all in the family," Selma added with a sly wink.

"Where *is* my father?" Nina demanded. "If you removed his mind from his body to make room for Bryan's, what did you do with his brain?"

"I still have it," Bryan said proudly. "It's on disc."

"What?" Selma cried in surprise. "I told you to erase it! That's evidence that could be used against us!"

"Don't worry, my darling," Bryan said calmly. "No one will find it. Just like no one will find his nosy little daughter."

Nina's throat tightened as she saw Bryan reach for the main control pad. In just a few seconds, her body would be ripped apart into trillions of microscopic pieces.

"Freeze!" a voice shouted from somewhere in the room. "Back away from those controls and put your hands in the air!"

As Selma and Bryan turned slowly around, Nina ran up to the Plexiglas window and saw six uniformed security officers holding their stun guns on the murderous couple.

"What took you so long!" Nina shouted. Before going to the Gridleys, she'd placed an anonymous call to Base Security reporting unauthorized use of the Transmatter. At the time, she'd hoped that her call would merely lead to an investigation of the Gridleys' activities. She had no idea her call would end up saving her own life!

Now, her terror turning to rage, Nina looked out at the Gridleys and steeled herself. "All right, you two," she said coldly. "Now where's my father?"

■ ■ ■ ■

Just like he had boasted, Bryan Gridley had Brendan Chung's electronically coded brain on a computer disc. In exchange for a lighter sentence, he and his wife agreed to reverse the process

89

and, using the Transmatter, they re-transplanted Brendan Chung's mind back into his body. When Nina saw her father whole once more, she broke down crying. Her father had no idea why his daughter was so upset—for he had no memory at all of the time he had been "missing."

As for Bryan Gridley, his brain was reduced to millions of electronic bits and recorded onto a computer disc. There it would remain forever, his consciousness doomed to drift through eternity locked in a single moment of murderous rage.

the beacon

During the first five months of 1855, seven merchant ships were destroyed on the rocky shoals south of Gull Point, Maine. All of these shipwrecks occurred at night, many of them in less than ideal weather. Although bits and pieces of the doomed sailing vessels were later recovered, not one piece of cargo was ever found. Nor were any bodies. In all, 152 sailors and the nearly $500,000 in precious cargo appeared to have simply vanished into thin air.

The citizens of Gull Point had many explanations for these mysterious shipwrecks. Some people blamed the tricky winds that whipped across the area's steep granite cliffs, suggesting they blew the ships off-course, smashed them against the rocks, and then carried the resulting debris out to sea. Others charged that the town's ancient, wood-burning lighthouse was simply inadequate, that the doomed crews got lost and ended up grounding themselves trying to spot it. Still other people had a more frightening and fanciful explanation for these disasters: a sea monster.

The story currently circulating around Gull Point was that a huge, squidlike creature was lurking offshore. When a ship was unfortunate enough to enter its territory, the beast would rise up, grab the vessel in its 30-foot-long tentacles, and hurl it against the rocky shoals like an ape cracking open a coconut against a palm tree. Then it would scoop out the ship's insides, dropping man and cargo alike down its gigantic gullet. Only when its voracious appetite was satisfied would it disappear back into the murky depths from which it had come.

Having recently celebrated his fourteenth birthday, Charlie Montooth considered himself far too old to believe such wild stories. He long ago learned there was no Santa Claus, no Easter Bunny, and no Tooth Fairy. To him, an educated boy living in the middle of the nineteenth century, the idea of sea monsters seemed like nothing more than ignorant superstition.

Yet his father seemed to like the sea monster explanation. "The sea holds many mysteries," the older man was fond of saying. "We landlubbers would be fools to think we understood all the powers of the deep."

Charlie wondered if his father truly believed in killer sea monsters, or if the man was just afraid to blame the lighthouse. After all, Charlie's father was the town's lighthouse keeper, a position he'd held for over 25 years. Every day, the man would haul wood cut from the local forest up 335 winding stairs to the top of the brick and masonry tower that stood at the very edge of Gull Point Harbor. There he'd set these logs atop a bed of kindling he'd laid down earlier that morning. When the sun set, he'd set a kerosene-soaked torch to the kindling, and within minutes the beacon fire would be ablaze. Its brilliance would dance off a polished aluminum reflector, making it visible for many miles out to sea.

The talk around town was that the old lighthouse would soon get one of the new gas-burning lamps that had become so popular along the New England seaboard recently. But change was slow to come to Gull Point, and until a modern gaslamp could be installed, it was up to Charlie's dad to keep the beacon burning through wind, rain, fog, and sleet. It was a job in which he took great pride, and he refused to consider that the light he produced could somehow be inadequate for approaching ships.

"There's nothing wrong with *my* lighthouse," Charlie's father stubbornly insisted. "For decades, it's brought ships into port safe and sound. If all of a sudden ships are wrecking themselves on the rocks, something else has to be responsible. And a sea monster seems as good an explanation as any."

Charlie wanted to believe his dad, but the sea monster explanation just seemed so, well, far-fetched. As painful as it might be to admit, Charlie knew that the lighthouse itself may have played some role in these recent disasters.

But Charlie's father stood firm, and when the company that insured four of the seven lost ships stepped forward and offered a $1,000 reward to anyone who could provide solid information as to the cause of the wrecks or the fate of their crews, the man saw a golden opportunity to prove his point.

"We're going to get that sea monster," Charlie's father declared as the Montooth family sat down to a fresh seafood dinner that evening in the kitchen of their small brick cottage that stood right at the base of the lighthouse. "We're going to collect the thousand dollar reward. And we're going to prove there's nothing wrong with my lighthouse."

"Amos, you're talking crazy," Charlie's mother said. "Everyone knows there's no such thing as sea monsters."

"We'll see about that," Charlie's dad said as he slurped down a mouthful of his wife's homemade clam chowder. "When we bring the body of that beast to shore, a harpoon stuck through its black heart, then we'll see who believes in what."

"What do you mean, when *we* bring the body to shore?" Charlie asked warily.

"I mean you and me, son," his dad said. "You can't expect me to go monster hunting all by myself. At the very least it's a two-man job."

"You are *not* taking my son on your crazy monster hunt!" Charlie's mother protested. "He's just a child!"

"I am not!" Charlie found himself insisting. The last thing he wanted to be called was a *child*. "I'm fourteen years old. I'm a young man. And I'm going out with dad—if only to prove to him that he's wrong."

"I think you're both crazy," his mother said. "But if you're both bound and determined to do this, then I suppose there's no way to stop you."

"Don't worry, Mom, I'll be fine," Charlie assured her. "We both know there's no such thing as sea monsters. But maybe we'll find what's *really* causing these wrecks—and end up a thousand dollars richer!"

■ ■ ■ ■

For three entire weeks, Charlie and his father trolled the waters north and south of Gull Point in the family sailboat for any sign of the ocean beast his father still insisted was behind the series of unexplained shipwrecks. Apparently, they weren't the only

94

ones who'd heard about the $1,000 reward, or who thought they might collect it by bagging a monster squid, for that first week at least two dozen other boats were in the water with them.

But by the second week, that number had dwindled to an even dozen, and by week three, they found themselves practically alone in the choppy coastal waters. Strangely, during this entire time, there was not a single shipwreck anywhere in the area. Charlie's dad was certain there was a connection.

"This beast is a crafty fellow," he said as they sailed through the rough seas. "He knows we're looking for him. He's laying low until he feels it's safe to strike again."

"So now we're not only looking for the biggest squid in the world, but also the smartest," Charlie said with obvious sarcasm. "I think maybe you've been out at sea just a little too long, Dad."

"Oh, he's out here," his father said with a grin. "You can count on it."

Charlie didn't believe his dad any more than he had when this whole crazy expedition started, but as he traveled up and down Maine's southern coast, the mystery of the shipwrecks began to gnaw deeper and deeper at his gut. He wanted to know why these ships and their crews were disappearing virtually without a trace, not just so he could collect the $1,000 reward, but so he could go to sleep without fear that some horrible presence was lurking just offshore.

But although they covered nearly fifteen miles that afternoon, they saw no sign of a sea monster or anything else that could account for the recent shipwrecks. As sunset approached, the Montooths finally turned back toward home. Charlie's father was still responsible for operating the lighthouse, and much work remained to be done before darkness fell.

"I'm going to go out for one last look, Dad," Charlie said as he dropped his father off at the dock beneath the lighthouse. Although he still refused to believe that the sea monster was real, the fact was he'd much rather spend his time on the water than helping his father carry heavy logs up 335 stairs.

"All right, but if you catch sign of him, get back here as quickly as you can. Don't try to take him on yourself," his father instructed. "And don't stay out long. Looks like a squall's moving in. Should be here in another hour or two."

Charlie looked to the northeast and saw that, indeed, a line of dark clouds had formed on the horizon.

"I'll be back by dusk," he promised, then pushed the boat away from the dock and headed back out to sea.

■ ■ ■ ■

The storm hit far sooner than Charlie had expected. It began with a chilly wind from the northeast, which was joined by a light spray which soon turned into a heavy rain.

Charlie tried to turn his sailboat back to Gull Point Harbor, but the wind seemed determined to stop him as it blew him further and further to the south. Soon, darkness settled on the open sea, and Charlie found himself badly disoriented, not knowing which way to steer his small, fragile craft.

And then, like a beacon of hope, he saw a fiery glow nearly dead ahead.

"The lighthouse!" he cried aloud, and turned his boat to head directly toward what he believed to be his father's light. Between his sail and rudder, he somehow managed to tack against the fierce, shifting wind and make headway toward the lifesaving beacon.

But then, just as the shoreline became visible through the murky haze, he heard a terrible groan and felt the small boat pitch wildly as it slammed into a row of undersea rocks. As he went spinning into the icy water, Charlie realized, much to his horror, that he was nowhere near Gull Point Harbor. He was at least three miles south of town, on the rocky shoals that had been the site of the first mysterious shipwreck.

But what about that light? he wondered. If it wasn't the lighthouse, then what was it?

Coughing and sputtering, Charlie swam like a young man possessed, the mysterious light still visible near the shoreline. Carried along by the powerful current, he continued to drift south until the water became shallow enough so that he could walk the rest of the way to the shore. Soaked to the skin, he dragged himself up onto a scrub-covered bluff overlooking the small grotto near where his boat had crashed. He recognized this place as Chesterson's Cove. Barely visible from the surrounding cliffs, it was virtually inaccessible from the sea because of the treacherous rock formations that stood immediately offshore.

Reaching the rim of the cove, Charlie looked down to see a stunning sight. At least two dozen men were down on the beach below stoking a huge bonfire. They were singing and drinking and apparently having a wild celebration of some kind.

And then, even as Charlie continued to watch in awe, he saw the shape of a huge three-masted schooner suddenly materialize out of the mists a quarter-mile out to sea. The powerful sailing vessel was heading straight for them, its bow bouncing up and down as it was tossed violently about by the storm-driven surf.

It was then that Charlie understood what was happening. There was a monster at work here, all right. But it wasn't a giant squid or any other mindless denizen of the deep. This monster

97

was the most cunning creature on the face of the earth—and his name was Man. The people below had set this fire deliberately to confuse merchant ships, to make their captains *think* that they were heading for Gull Point Harbor. Instead, they were being *lured* into Chesterson's Cove—and the rocks that would spell their doom.

"They're pirates!" Charlie gasped, just before he heard a thunderous *crash* as the bow of the incoming ship slammed into the jagged rocks at the northern entrance to Chesterson's Cove. This was followed by another *crash* and the groan of twisting wood as the mighty ship proceeded to tear itself apart on the rocky barrier.

As a group, the pirates swarmed toward the sinking vessel, firing their pistols at any of the sailors who so much as dared to show any resistance.

I've got to report this to the police! Charlie thought urgently. Now I can collect that thousand dollar reward!

Moving at top speed, Charlie sprinted nearly two miles through the rain and sleet until, chilled to the bone, he stumbled into Cape McClane, the small coastal town south of Gull Point.

Running up to the door of the Cape McClane police headquarters, he shouted, "Help! Someone, help me!"

A gaslight flicked on in the window above the station's main entrance. Then Charlie saw shadows moving above, followed by the sound of boots coming down wooden stairs. Within seconds, a lock turned, and Captain Stearman, a thin, ruddy-faced man whose skin was deeply creased by forty New England winters, appeared at the door.

"Why, you're Amos Montooth's boy, aren't you?" he said, recognizing Charlie. "What are you doing out in this weather? Don't you know what time it is?"

"Pirates!" Charlie managed to choke out. "They're over at Chesterson's Cove! They're drawing ships onto the rocks and killing the crews! We have to stop them!"

For a long moment, the craggy police captain considered the youth standing before him and his wild claims. Without changing expression, he said, "Stay right there," then he disappeared back into the building.

■ ■ ■ ■

An hour later, Charlie Montooth, Captain Stearman, and two dozen heavily-armed deputies galloped on horseback along the road to Chesterson's Cove. On Captain Stearman's orders, Charlie waited on the cliffs above as the lawmen charged down into the grotto, catching the pirates by surprise and engaging them in a field rifle battle. When the dust cleared, fifteen buccaneers were under arrest, while another eight lay dead in the sand. Only four of Stearman's men were injured.

"You did well, boy," Captain Stearman said proudly as his deputies marched the surviving pirates back toward Cape McClane. "Now these shores are safe once again. I'll be sure to put a good word in for you about that thousand dollar reward. You earned it. Now let's get you home where you belong."

Eager to tell his father about his victory, Charlie mounted the horse the police chief had loaned him and prepared to ride back to Gull Point. But before moving off, he took one last glance back at Chesterson Cove and the remains of the bloody battle which had just occurred. The last embers of the pirates' bonfire were beginning to burn out, and beyond that, on the rocks offshore, lay the broken remains of the doomed merchant ship the thieves had tried to plunder.

And then something else caught Charlie's eye. Farther out in the ocean, a large, oval shape seemed to rise out of the water. Just as the moon broke out from behind the thinning storm clouds, a ray of silvery light struck the object, and for a brief moment, Charlie thought he saw an eye—an eye as large as a full-grown man—looking back at him.

Charlie prepared to speak, to call Stearman's attention to the horrific sight, but before he could utter a word, the mysterious form dipped back beneath the waves and vanished in the darkness.

Trying to shake off the creepy feeling that now chilled him to the bone, Charlie kicked his horse forward and started riding toward the brilliant beacon of light to the north that was his father's lighthouse. There he would tell his father the whole fantastic story—but with no mention of sea monsters.

a lotto murder

A dramatic drum roll signaled the broadcast of the winning Lotto numbers. "And now, ladies and gentlemen," the tuxedoed announcer declared, "the holder of tonight's twenty million dollar Lotto jackpot prize is! . . ."

Alexis Noguchi sat on the edge of her bed staring intently with wide eyes at the twelve-inch color TV glowing brightly before her. Although at age thirteen she was far too young to legally play her state's weekly lottery, her parents always bought a one-dollar ticket just prior to each Wednesday's drawing, and counted on her to keep track of the results. Now, nervously biting her lower lip, she clutched this week's ticket and set about imagining what she and her parents could do with a cool twenty mil.

On the TV, six numbered Ping-Pong balls were spit out of a machine that looked something like a giant gumball dispenser. The numbered balls rolled into a clear plastic tube. When the weekly ritual was complete, the announcer—whose hair seemed to be slipping a little to the left—read the winning combination.

"Tonight's Super Lotto numbers are five, twelve, fourteen, twenty-six, thirty-three, and fifty!" he said.

Her hands trembling, Alexis stared down at the six-number combination on the ticket. It read: 4-13-20-22-32-40. Not even close. Not even one number right.

"If you're a winner, our heartiest congratulations!" the announcer said, wearing a big phony smile. "And if you're not, be sure to play again next week. With just a little bit of luck, our next Super Lotto jackpot winner could be—!"

Before the man could even finish his sentence, Alexis snapped off the TV. Then she crumbled the losing ticket into a ball and tossed it into the trash can, the same one into which she had tossed every other losing lottery ticket she'd had for the past five years.

"A little bit of luck, my eye!" she snarled. She knew that the odds of hitting all six numbers—even out of order—were something like fourteen million to one. Even guessing five out of six numbers, which won you a lesser cash prize, was about as unlikely as giving birth to quadruplets. With chances like those, Alexis had to wonder how *anyone* ever managed to win. Not only had her own family never even gotten close, but she didn't know anyone else who had either. Hitting the jackpot was one of those things that always happened to strangers.

Alexis was about to go downstairs and give her folks the bad news when she heard what sounded like shouting coming from next door. This was not all that unusual. Their next door neighbors, Mr. and Mrs. Faber, were a retired couple who tended to fight just about every night. It had gotten so Alexis came to regard their shouts and shrieks as just another part of the city's background noise. But tonight, the level of verbal violence seemed higher than normal. The Fabers seemed to be going at each other with everything they had. If Alexis didn't know them better, she might think that they were about to kill each other.

Curious, Alexis got her father's binoculars from the hall closet, then came back to her room and focused them on the house next door, specifically at the glowing kitchen window. There she caught glimpses of the older couple wildly waving their arms about as they screamed at each other at the top of their lungs.

As Alexis continued to watch, Mrs. Faber turned and stormed out of the kitchen. Mr. Faber was right behind her. A moment later, there was a loud *bang!* Then an awful silence filled the air, making Alexis's blood run cold.

■ ■ ■ ■

"I think Mr. Faber shot Mrs. Faber!" Alexis cried fearfully as she ran into the family room where her mother and father were watching the end of a rental movie. "Or maybe *Mrs.* Faber shot *Mr.* Faber! Either way, we've got to do something!"

"Whoa! Whoa! Slow down, Alexis," her father said, easing himself off the leather couch. "What are you talking about?"

Alexis quickly told her parents about everything she'd seen and heard next door. "Someone's been killed over there," she cried. "I'm sure of it!"

Her parents looked at each other with deep concern. Although Alexis was as imaginative as most thirteen-year-olds, she was not known for making up stories or jumping to wild conclusions. Clearly, *something* out of the ordinary had gone on next door. But what?

"Maybe we should call them up and make sure everything's okay," her mother suggested.

Alexis fidgeted nervously as her father looked up the Fabers' number in their address book, then punched the combination into their cordless telephone. A moment later, someone answered at the other end.

"Mr. Faber? This is Harry Noguchi next door," Alexis's father said, throwing his daughter an anxious glance. "Sorry to bother you so late at night, but my daughter heard what she thought might be a gunshot coming from your house. We wanted to make sure that everyone was all right." He continued to maintain eye contact with Alexis as he listened to Mr. Faber's reply. "I see. Is it possible for me to speak with Mrs. Faber? Oh, I see. Uh-huh. All right. Well, sorry again for calling so late. Have a nice evening." With that, he returned the cordless handset to its cradle.

"Well?" Alexis demanded.

"Mr. Faber says everything is fine," her father replied, a hint of irritation in his voice. "He thinks the 'gunshot' you heard might have been the backfire from a passing car. He says he heard it, too."

"And what about *Mrs.* Faber?" Alexis asked. "Did you get to speak with her?"

"Mr. Faber said she was, well, *indisposed*," her father said, somewhat embarrassed. "I think the best thing to do is just forget this whole thing ever happened."

Alexis had been around long enough to know that when someone was "indisposed," it usually meant that he or she was in the bathroom. But under these circumstances, she figured it could mean something else: Like *Mrs. Faber is dead.*

And so, despite what Mr. Faber had told her father, Alexis vowed not to rest until she was convinced that both her neighbors were indeed alive and well.

■ ■ ■ ■

The next day, when Alexis returned home from school, she went straight up to her bedroom and glanced over at the Faber house next door. From her second-story window, she could clearly see Mr. Faber in his fenced-in backyard. Dressed in work clothes, he was down on his hands and knees, doing something with his flower garden. This immediately struck Alexis as very strange. In the past, it had been *Mrs.* Faber who she usually saw doing all the gardening. In fact, Alexis had never seen Mr. Faber do any kind of yard work except mow the lawn and occasionally trim the hedges. Something was definitely up.

Convinced that the authorities had to be alerted, but not wanting to embarrass herself in case she was wrong, she looked up the police department's non-emergency number in the phone book and punched it into her telephone. Unlike the 911 system, which automatically revealed the caller's number and address to the police, the non-emergency line would not be able to trace her call.

Lowering her voice in an attempt to disguise her identity, she quickly said, "Um, I'd like to report a possible murder at 6172 Lockerbee Lane." Then she slammed the handset back into its cradle.

Gasping for air, like she'd just run a marathon, Alexis knew that she had just passed the point of no return. If she was right—if Mr. Faber *was* a murderer—then she had just done all of society a great favor. But if she was wrong—if Mr. Faber was an innocent man—then she could be in the worst trouble of her life.

Just then a car pulled up next door. Running to her window, Alexis saw that it was a police cruiser. They had responded to her emergency call and were going to check up on the mysterious Mr. Faber.

Wanting to hear everything that was said, Alexis grabbed her basketball from her closet, raced downstairs and out to the front driveway, and began shooting hoops against the backboard mounted above their garage. Here, between the slapping sounds made by the ball bouncing off the hard asphalt, she could pick up bits and pieces of the conversation next door as the police officers interviewed Mr. Faber on his doorstep.

"My wife was fine when she left this morning," Mr. Faber told the officers.

"Then you're telling me she's not home now?" the female officer inquired.

"No, she's gone to visit her sister," Mr. Faber replied. "Why are you interested? Is something wrong?"

"Someone called us inquiring about her well-being," the male officer replied somewhat cryptically.

"That's odd," Mr. Faber said with concern.

"Do you have a number at her sister's?" the female officer asked while taking notes.

"I do, but I don't think anyone will be there," Mr. Faber said. "They were going to rent a houseboat and spend some time on Lake Shelbourne, so they won't be reachable by phone." He hesitated for a moment. "I do expect her to call in from time to time, though."

"Well, when your wife does call, could you ask her to please give us a call as well?" the first officer requested. She handed Mr. Faber a business card.

"No problem," Mr. Faber said cheerfully. "To tell you the truth, after this visit, I'm kinda worried about her myself."

The officers nodded, mumbled something about "false alarms," then returned to their car.

Alexis was furious. The man was lying through his teeth and she knew it. His story about his wife renting a houseboat with her sister was so feeble an explanation even a TV detective would see through it. Yes, it was clear to Alexis that she was going to have to call the police again—*after* she got some proof.

■ ■ ■ ■

About an hour after the police officers' visit, Mr. Faber backed his mid-sized four-door sedan out of his two-car garage, turned onto the street, then rolled slowly off. Before the garage door automatically closed, Alexis noticed that Mrs. Faber's car, a late-model American-made coupe, was still inside. That meant that if Mrs. Faber *had* gone to visit her sister, she hadn't driven there.

Hoping that Mr. Faber wouldn't return too soon, Alexis quickly headed over to inspect Mr. Faber's fenced-in backyard. There, using a small gardening spade she'd taken from her family's toolshed, she began carefully digging around the small flower bed Mr. Faber had been puttering around in earlier that afternoon.

Five minutes later, she'd already come upon something very interesting. At first, it looked like nothing more than a piece of shiny metal. But as Alexis lifted it out of the ground and brushed away the mud, she was shocked to see that it was actually a wedding band.

"He *did* kill her!" Alexis gasped. Then a sick feeling came over her. Where, she wondered, was the body?

Just then, Alexis heard Mr. Faber's garage door opening. *He's back!* her mind screamed. If he comes back here and catches me digging through his garden, I'm dead!

Looking around frantically for an escape route, Alexis saw that the only way back to her house was along the row of hedges—which would take her right past the Fabers' garage. Mr. Faber was sure to see her that way, so she had to think of something else.

And then her eyes came to rest on the Fabers' basement windows, one of which was cranked open. Moving swiftly, Alexis ran over to the window and pried it all the way open. Then, taking a deep breath, she lowered herself feetfirst into the dark, dank room.

"Oh, no! . . ." she gasped aloud when she saw what was at her feet. The basement's concrete floor was stained dark red. The liquid that had collected around the drainage grate in the middle of the room still glistened moistly. *It's blood!* Alexis thought in terror. This must be where Mr. Faber killed his wife!

Just then, she heard the floorboards overhead creak as someone walked around in the home above her. Realizing that with Mr. Faber in the house she might be able to sneak back across the yard unseen, she decided to climb back out the window. But as she turned, she accidentally knocked into an old lamp, which fell to the concrete floor with a resounding *crash!*

"Who's there?" she heard Mr. Faber call from upstairs. "Who's down in the basement?"

Before Alexis could move, the basement door swung open and Mr. Faber came thundering down the wooden stairs, a baseball bat clutched firmly in his hands. He stopped in surprise when he saw Alexis standing on the crate by the window.

"Alexis? What are you doing down here, young lady?" he asked sternly.

"I know what you did," Alexis found herself saying. "I know that you killed your wife."

"I did *what*?" the old man gasped.

"I heard the gunshot last night," Alexis stated, now having no choice but to try to make the man confess. "And I found this buried in your garden." She held up the gold band she'd found in the flowerbed, then pointed at the red-stained floor. "This is where you killed her, isn't it, Mr. Faber?"

"What the heck are you talking about?" Mr. Faber demanded, clearly offended by Alexis's charges.

"It's blood—" Alexis began, pointing again to the red-stained floor.

"It's *paint*, you silly girl!" Mr. Faber snapped. "I had some left in a can from years ago, and I accidentally kicked it over while I was rearranging things down here last weekend." He flipped on the light. "See for yourself."

"Okay, then what about the ring?" Alexis countered, not even bothering to look at the dried paint.

"It's *mine*!" Mr. Faber growled, holding up his ringless left hand. "Edna's had me on a diet for the past month. I've lost so much weight that my fingers got skinny, and it must have slipped off while I was gardening. I've been looking for it everywhere! Thanks for finding it. Now get out of here."

He snatched the ring from Alexis's finger, and slipped it onto his own left hand.

"Okay, well . . ." Alexis stammered, feeling more foolish by the second. "If your wife is alive, then where is she?"

"Up at Lake Shelbourne with her sister," Mr. Faber replied impatiently. "She's been planning this trip for weeks. She hates to drive, so she took the bus first thing this morning. I'm supposed to meet her up there in a few days—as soon as I pick up our check."

"What check?" Alexis asked.

"We won last night's Mega Lotto," Mr. Faber said, smiling for the first time. "We didn't exactly hit the jackpot, but we did get five out of six numbers. And that was good for half a million! Boy, you should have heard us screaming when we realized we'd won. Edna got so excited, she broke out the champagne we'd been saving for our fiftieth wedding anniversary."

Now Alexis *really* felt like a fool. The screams she'd heard the night before weren't from a fight, but from a celebration. And the gunshot? Only the popping of a champagne cork.

"Well, uh, congratulations, Mr. Faber," Alexis said, her face now bright red with embarrassment as she slunk toward the basement stairway. "I'm really happy for you. And Mrs. Faber. I never knew anyone who ever won the lottery before."

"It's a good feeling, let me tell you," Mr. Faber said, still grinning wildly. "You should play it when you get old enough."

But Alexis wasn't listening anymore. She was too busy being furious with herself for thinking such terrible things about a nice old man like Mr. Faber. Even worse, she'd called him a murderer right to his face! She wondered how she'd ever be able to face him again.

Alexis was just about to exit the basement when she noticed something caught in the doorjamb. Reaching down she pulled out a scrap of cotton fabric. Its tight polka dot pattern seemed strangely familiar to her. And then she remembered where she'd seen it. It was from the dress Mrs. Faber had worn the previous night—the last time Alexis had seen the woman alive. Now, looking closer at the scrap, she saw that its edges were darkly stained—the color of dried blood. The story about the ring—the paint—Mr. Faber *had* been lying, just like he'd lied to the police!

Spinning around, Alexis looked back at Mr. Faber, who was still holding the baseball bat. He eyed the piece of bloody fabric in her hand, and the giddy smile vanished from his face. Now he looked *very* serious—*dead* serious, in fact.

"A half a million dollars is a lot of money," he said in a low, measured voice. "It's even more when you get to spend it all by yourself—don't you think?"

Too frightened to even scream, Alexis turned and began to run. But as she did, her foot slipped on the top step, she lost her balance and went crashing backward down the steps, landing painfully at Mr. Faber's feet.

"Guess you won't get a chance to play Lotto after all, Alexis," Mr. Faber said, raising the baseball bat high above his head. " 'Cause your luck has just run out."

live and learn

osh Kimlan couldn't believe the good news. A new Fine Arts High School was about to open in his district, and as an eighth grader, he could start there as a freshman the following fall. To Josh this sounded almost too good to be true. The truth was he was mediocre in math. His science was substandard. And in English his grades were, in his own words, "sucky." But a school that taught art, music, and drama? Ah, now *there* he could be a star!

"I've got to go to that new high school," Josh told his parents over supper. "You know how much I love music and acting. It's the perfect place for me!"

"If that's where you want to go, we certainly have no objection," his father replied. "But I hear you have to meet

113

certain academic standards to get in. After all, I'm sure just about *every* student in the city would want to go to that school if they could."

"Uh, what kind of 'standards'?" Josh asked warily.

"I hear you have to have a 3.0 grade point average or better," his mother said.

"And if your GPA ever drops below that, you're out of the school," his father added.

Suddenly the chicken and mashed potatoes lying on Josh's plate didn't look nearly as appetizing as they did just a moment ago. The fact was, Josh's grade point average was only 2.6. To get it up to a 3.0 by the end of the school year, he'd have to get just about straight A's on his next three report cards. That would mean working harder than he'd ever worked in his life. And even then, there was no guarantee that he'd actually get the kinds of grades he needed.

Completely depressed, Josh didn't even do that night's homework and instead spent the rest of the evening listening to his favorite CDs.

The next day, Josh checked with his homeroom teacher and learned that his parents were right about the new Fine Arts High School's academic requirements. All day long, Josh asked himself how he could ever achieve this seemingly impossible goal.

A glimmer of hope appeared during his afternoon math class when his teacher passed back a test they'd taken a few days earlier. As usual, he got a C, but he noticed that the boy next to him, Cary Lassitar, had gotten an A. This was not at all like Cary. For as long as he'd known him, Cary had been an even worse student than Josh himself. Well, if Cary Lassitar can earn A's, Josh thought, so can I!

After class, Josh intercepted Cary in the hallway. "Hey, congratulations on that A you got today," he said cheerfully.

"Thanks, Josh," Cary responded with a proud smile.

"So how'd you do it?" Josh asked. "I mean, I've never seen you get an A in math before. What's your secret?"

"Uh, I don't know," Cary replied, suddenly very nervous. "Just got lucky I guess. Uh, look, I gotta get to gym. I'll see you around, okay?"

Grabbing his books, his eyes cast toward the floor, Cary dashed away.

He's hiding something, Josh thought. Maybe he cheated and is afraid of getting caught. Well, however he managed to get that A, I doubt he'll be able to do it again.

But Cary *did* do it again. And again after that. Over the next two weeks, Cary Lassitar got an A on every test he took and every homework assignment he handed in. And these weren't just mid-level A's. They were one hundred percent perfect A-plus grades every time!

Josh, on the other hand, never managed to get better than a B-minus. Although he was bound and determined to raise his average so he could qualify for Fine Arts High, he couldn't even come close to performing like Cary. It just didn't seem fair. What did Cary have that he didn't?

He's doing something sneaky to get such perfect grades, Josh thought, eyeing Cary across his math class. But he can't just be cheating. There's no way he could get away with that all the time. No, he's doing something else. And I've got to find out what it is.

Obsessed with learning Cary's secret, Josh followed the boy home from school that day, making sure to stay at least half a block behind him so he wouldn't be noticed.

Cary's house turned out to be a one-story, ranch-style home at the end of a quiet residential street lined with huge oak trees. On the sidewalk sat several boxes filled with old, discarded pieces of computer equipment. Josh knew that Cary's dad was somehow involved in electronics, and figured this trash had belonged to him.

Keeping his head low and moving as quietly as he could, Josh crept along the side of the house, bobbing up and peering quickly into each window until he located Cary's bedroom. Then, carefully peering over the window ledge, he saw something extremely puzzling.

Cary was seated at his desk facing what appeared to be a sophisticated home computer. Connected to it was a metal box about the size of a portable TV. Josh had spent many an afternoon hanging around his local computer superstore, checking out the cool games and the hardware needed to run them, but he'd never before seen a unit that looked anything like the thing on Cary's desk.

What the heck could *that* be? he wondered.

After booting up the computer, Cary picked up what looked like a pair of oversized goggles connected to the mystery box by a length of thick cable. He placed these goggles over his eyes, then sat back in his chair.

It must be some new kind of virtual reality system, Josh thought. Cool!

As Josh continued to watch in awe, images began to flash by on the computer screen. At first they seemed to involve mathematical formulas, but after a while, they shifted to pictures from American history. Specifically, they were pictures from the Civil War—which just happened to be the period they were studying at school.

Now, Josh had worked with computerized study aids before. In fact, his parents had been so desperate to get his grades up that they'd bought him nearly a dozen different educational programs over the last two years. Most of them were a lot of fun to play with, but did little to actually boost his classroom performance. Could this system be different? Was it possible that something about learning information through virtual reality was better than just getting words and pictures off a regular computer screen?

Josh got his answer the next afternoon when Cary gave a flawless oral report on the Battle of Gettysburg to their history class. Josh recognized many of the events Cary described as being from the images that had been on his computer screen the previous afternoon. Not only had Cary become familiar with the battle as a whole, but somehow he'd also managed to memorize countless numbers of names, dates, and other statistics with amazing detail.

Josh was clearly impressed.

After class, Josh cornered Cary by his locker. Keeping his voice low, he said, "I know how you're getting those A's."

"What are you talking about?" Cary replied, avoiding eye contact with Josh as he arranged the books in his locker.

"I'm talking about the computer," Josh pressed on. "You know, that virtual reality gizmo you have in your bedroom."

"How did you find out?" Cary whispered harshly, his eyes suddenly filled with terror. "No one's supposed to know about that! It's top secret!"

"No one *will* know—if you share it with me," Josh assured him sugar-sweetly.

"I—I can't do that," Cary stammered. "The system's being developed by my dad's company. He brought a copy home for beta testing, to see how it works on ordinary people."

"It looks to me like it works great," Josh noted.

"But it's still in the testing stages," Cary insisted. "Dad's company wants to keep the technology top secret until they're ready to sell it. That way they can keep other companies from ripping them off. They don't even want anyone else to know such a machine even *exists!*"

"I told you, Cary, your secret is safe with me," Josh repeated. His friend gave an audible sigh of relief. "Just let me use it to get my grades high enough to get into the Fine Arts High School."

"If my dad catches me letting you use it, I tell you, he'll kill me," Cary groaned.

"And if you *don't* let me use it, I'll tell what I know to every newspaper in the city," Josh threatened. "I'm sure they would just *love* to know all about a machine that turns people into little geniuses."

"All right! All right!" Cary relented. "Come over to my place right after school. You know where I live?"

"You bet I do, *friend,*" Josh replied with a cold smile.

■ ■ ■ ■

"So what subject you want to start with first?" Cary asked Josh as he sat in front of his bedroom computer.

"Math," Josh replied without missing a beat. "That's always been my weakest subject."

"All right, I'll give you the ninth grade program, just to start you out easy," Cary said, clicking a command on the computer screen. Then he fit the goggles over Josh's eyes. "How does it feel?"

"I can't see anything," Josh said, jerking his head from side to side.

"You're not supposed to yet," Cary told him. "Now, you might feel a little lightheaded when the session's over, but that feeling will go away in a minute or so. Ready?"

"Okay, crank 'er up, Cary," Josh said eagerly, settling back in the chair.

"Now keep your eyes open and try to clear your mind," Cary said. "This will only take a minute."

Josh did as he had been instructed. A moment later, he saw hundreds of colored lights flashing in front of his eyes. Although the display was absolutely beautiful, there didn't seem to be any purpose or pattern to it. This went on for a short time, then Cary tapped Josh on the shoulder, "Okay, Josh," he said. "You can take off the goggles now. It's over."

Josh ripped the goggles off his face, sat up, and immediately felt slightly dizzy. "That's it?" he said, puzzled. "But I didn't see anything. There weren't any pictures or anything, just lights. How could I learn anything from *that*?"

"This machine doesn't teach you in the regular way," Cary explained. "It transmits information through the optic nerve directly into the brain. It's kind of like sending information from one computer to another through different telephone lines."

"But I don't feel any smarter," Josh said uneasily. "In fact, I don't feel any different at all."

"What's the square root of four hundred and thirty-six?" Cary asked.

Under normal circumstances, Josh would have just sat there with a blank look on his face. But now he responded without hesitation, "Twenty point eighty-eight." He was startled by his lightning-fast response. "Wow! quick, hit me with another question! A hard one!"

"If Joe's car gets twenty-four miles to the gallon, and it has a sixteen gallon tank, how many stops will he have to make to drive three thousand miles?"

"Eight," Josh replied as easily as if he'd just been asked his age. "And he'd have exactly three gallons left over."

Cary gave Josh a glowing smile. Josh broke out laughing. He couldn't believe how smart he'd become in just a mere matter of seconds.

"More!" he shouted. "I want to learn more! I want to learn science and history and French. I want to know everything there is to know!"

"You have to take it slow," Cary warned him.

"Slow—*shmo!*" Josh cried excitedly. "I want knowledge!"

"Give your brain a chance to absorb all the new information," Cary insisted. "Remember, raw knowledge alone isn't enough. You also have to know what to do with it. Otherwise, it's nothing more than a bunch of disconnected information. At least, that's what my dad explained to me."

Josh agreed to take Cary's advice. He would take it slow . . . for now.

■　■　■　■

The following day, a chapter test was held in Josh's math class. As usual, Josh hadn't even bothered to glance at his textbook the night before.

However, this time, when the test was placed in front of him, Josh found the questions to be laughably simple. Although the class was given the entire forty-minute-long period to complete the exam, Josh had it finished in fifteen minutes. His grade was 100 percent. An A-plus.

After school, Josh returned to Cary's house, and this time he got programmed in cell biology. The next day, during science class, he rattled off words like "membrane," "nucleus," "osmosis," and "mitochondria" as if he'd used them in everyday conversation for years.

Day by day, week by week, his grade point average slowly rose. But all of the bad grades he got earlier in the year were still dragging his GPA down like lead weights pulling a hot air balloon toward earth.

Come spring, it appeared that his last chance to qualify for entry to Fine Arts High was the National Achievement Tests (NATs), which were given to eighth graders in late April. If he could score a 95 or above on a scale of 100, his earlier lackluster grades wouldn't matter, and his place at the Fine Arts High School would be all but guaranteed.

There was just one gigantic problem—the NATs were comprehensive, meaning they covered every subject from algebra to zoology for every class he'd taken to date. And Josh didn't believe he was ready to take on such a challenge without more "brain juice" from Cary's computer.

"I need everything your computer can give me," Josh told Cary as he sat himself down in front of what he called the "learning machine."

"You know I can't do that," Cary replied with a heavy sigh. "It's just not a good idea."

Josh ignored him. "Give me all you've got. Math. Science. History. Civics. The works!"

"But your brain won't be able to handle it, Josh," Cary began. "I'm afraid it will—"

"*I'll* worry about my brain!" Josh snapped. "I've handled everything you've given me so far. It's time to go for broke. Let's see what this baby can *do*! I mean, it's not like you have a choice, right? You don't want this wonder machine exposed to the world, do you?"

Cary smirked, then booted up his computer. "All right, Josh, you want it, you got it," he said. "Be prepared to get the brain boost of your life!

Already familiar with the routine, Josh slipped the goggles over his eyes, settled back, and prepared himself to become the smartest kid in the world.

■ ■ ■ ■

"Now remember, you have exactly one hour to complete the first portion of this test," the teacher said as he moved through the classroom passing out the blue test booklets to the nervous-looking students. "All the questions are multiple choice. If you find you're having a problem with any of them, move on and come back to it later. Remember, there is a penalty for incorrect answers, so don't guess. All right, is everyone ready? Then open your tests and—*begin!*"

Beaming with anticipation, Josh Kimlan read the first question:

The principal document that embodies the principles by which our nation is governed is called:

A) The Declaration of Independence
B) The Gettysburg Address
C) The Constitution
D) The Bill of Rights

"Easy, the Constitution," Josh said to himself, marking C on his answer form.

He continued to breeze through the test in this fashion until question twenty-five, *"Who was the President who authorized the Louisiana Purchase?"* Suddenly his eyes began to lose focus. It was like voices were speaking directly into his mind, giving the answers to questions he hadn't even read yet. Words and phrases like "New Deal," "Red Square," and "Four score and seven years ago—" kept echoing around inside his head without any rhyme or reason. The harder Josh tried to focus his thoughts, the more chaotic and formless they became.

And then, through the blast of mental white noise, Josh heard Cary Lassitar's words, "Raw knowledge alone isn't enough. You also have to know what to do with it. Otherwise, it's nothing but a bunch of disconnected information."

Tears welling up in his eyes, Josh wanted to turn the constant flow of information off, to flick the switch that would erase the countless gigabytes of data his brain had absorbed. But it was too late. He'd opened the floodgates—and now an entire encyclopedia's worth of knowledge was about to wash over him like an unstoppable tidal wave.

■ ■ ■ ■

"We don't know how long he'll be in this state," the psychiatrist said to Josh's parents as they viewed him through an inset window in the heavy wooden door a month after he'd been admitted to the psychiatric hospital. "We've tried everything we know, but we still haven't been able to get through to him."

"You mean, he just sits there like that talking to himself?" his father asked in disbelief.

"I'm afraid so," the doctor responded sadly.

"But how could something like this happen?" his mother demanded. "What caused his mind to shut down like that?"

"That's just the thing," the psychiatrist replied. "We don't believe his mind *has* shut down. It's more like it's stuck in overdrive. You should see the EKG results. We've never recorded such extreme brain activity in a patient before. I suspect he'll remain like this until either we find a way to slow the activity down, or his mind just, well, *burns out*."

Beyond the door, Josh Kimlan sat in a chair, his arms restrained by a straitjacket. As he stared blankly off into space, he spoke nonstop. "The square of the hypotenuse of a right triangle is equal to the sum of the squares of the other two sides ... The Magna Charta ... *Parlez-vous français?* ... One hundred and eighty-six thousand, two hundred and eighty-two miles per second ... Give me liberty, or give me death. ..."

COLLECT ALL THE SCARES YOU'VE EVER DREAMED
OF AT YOUR FAVORITE BOOKSTORE!

If you are unable to find these titles at your bookstore, fill in the Quantity Column for each title described, and order directly from Price Stern Sloan.

Mail order form to:
PUTNAM PUBLISHING GROUP
Mail Order Department
Department B
P.O. Box 12289
Newark, NJ 07101-5289

FAX   (201) 933-2316
☎   (800) 788-6262
☎   (201) 933-9292
On a touch-tone phone, hit prompt 1

Collect all the terrifying titles in the Scary Stories for Sleep-Overs series . . .

ISBN #	Quantity	Title	US price	Can. price
0-8431-2914-X	_____	Scary Stories for Sleep-Overs	$4.95	$6.50
0-8431-3451-8	_____	More Scary Stories for Sleep-Overs	$4.95	$6.50
0-8431-3588-3	_____	Still More Scary Stories for Sleep-Overs	$4.95	$6.50
0-8431-3746-0	_____	Even More Scary Stories for Sleep-Overs	$4.95	$6.50
0-8431-3915-3	_____	Super Scary Stories for Sleep-Overs	$4.95	$6.75
0-8431-3916-1	_____	More Super Scary Stories for Sleep-Overs	$4.95	$6.75
0-8431-8219-9	_____	Mega Scary Stories for Sleep-Overs	$5.95	$7.95

And check out the titles in this brand new scary and spine-tingling series . . .

ISBN #	Quantity	Title	US price	Can. price
0-8431-8220-2	_____	Scary Mysteries for Sleep-Overs	$5.95	$7.95
0-8431-8221-0	_____	More Scary Mysteries for Sleep-Overs	$5.95	$7.95
0-8431-7955-4	_____	Still More Scary Mysteries for Sleep-Overs	$6.95	$9.50
0-8431-7956-2	_____	Even More Scary Mysteries for Sleep-Overs	$6.95	$9.50

Now dive into NIGHTMARES! HOW WILL YOURS END? — Each title has over 20 endings!

ISBN #	Quantity	Title	US price	Can. price
0-8431-3862-9	_____	Castle of Horror	$4.50	$5.95
0-8431-3861-0	_____	Cave of Fear	$4.50	$5.95
0-8431-3860-2	_____	Planet of Terror	$4.50	$5.95
0-8431-3863-7	_____	Valley of the Screaming Statues	$4.50	$5.95

All orders must be prepaid in US funds

❏ Check or Money Order
❏ Visa
❏ Mastercard-Interbank
❏ American Express

Expiration Date _____

Signature _____

Daytime phone # _____

Postage/Handling Charges as follows:
$2.50 for first book
$0.75 each additional book
(Maximum shipping charge of $6.25)

Merchandise total	$_____
Shipping/Handling	$_____
Applicable Sales Tax (CA, NJ, NY, VA)	$_____
GST (Canada)	$_____
Total Amount (US currency only)	$_____

Minimum order $15.00
NOTE: Prices and handling charges are subject to change without notice, but we will always ship the least expensive edition available. Please allow 4 to 6 weeks for delivery.

Refer to source: SCARY